Raven

Raven

by

Trevor Ray and Jeremy Burnham

fantom
publishing

First published in 1977 in paperback by Corgi Books,
a division of Transworld Publishers, Ltd

This hardback edition published in 2014 by Fantom Films
fantomfilms.co.uk

A catalogue record for this book is available from the British Library.

Hardback edition ISBN: 978-1-78196-114-8

Typeset by Phil Reynolds Media Services, Leamington Spa
Printed and bound by CPI Group (UK) Ltd, Croydon, CR0 4YY

Jacket design by Stuart Manning

'Deep into the darkness peering,
Long I stood there, wondering, fearing,
Doubting, dreaming dreams no mortal
Ever dared to dream before...'

THE RAVEN
Edgar Allan Poe

Prologue

THE EARTHWORK MAZE LAY AT the top of the hill, the perfect spot for the midday break when working this far from the farmhouse. The old man killed the tractor diesel at the headland and sat for a moment, savouring the sudden quiet. One, three, six larks silvering the growing wind, the sounds of perfect silence…

He climbed stiffly up through the beech copse towards the ancient place, sun-filtered heat finding him through the high leaves. A dog barked across the valley, once, sharply, needing to prove that it was alive.

On May Eve, the village children still came this way at dusk with little screams of pretended fear, the boys ghosting among the trees, teasing the girls with the sounds of night. The Shepherds' Race among the flickering torches touched on inherited memory and stirred unknown terrors of unseen things within the minds of the young contestants. He climbed out into the full sun.

1

The maze lay above him still, encircling the earthwork at the summit. His contribution to the centuries was the few days he spent there each November during the fying and ditching time, tidying the earth banks, re-cutting the paths. It was work that satisfied as much as harvesting or ploughing, work that touched his boyhood and beyond.

The Raven stood braced against the sun, silky black at the entrance to the turf labyrinth.

He faced it, wondering what such a bird was doing visiting this rich inland country, a bird of the barren hills and craggy cliff. It turned and strutted away along the path.

He followed to the centre of the hilltop tumulus. Looking down into the shallow depression, into the centre of the maze, he saw the great black bird stand boldly beside the swaddled child... the sleeping foundling...

RAVEN.

Chapter One

THE TRAIN TORE OUT OF the tunnel, into the afternoon grey. Raven tossed aside the football magazine and waited for his eyes to adjust to the dull glare of the day. High above him, keeping pace with the snaking train, a hawk raced through the overcast sky.

The door of the compartment slid back and the ticket collector stared at the boy with hostility and suspicion. Raven grinned back, well aware that the sight of his feet resting on the opposite seat was causing the official a certain amount of pain.

'You got a ticket, son?'

Raven made a search through all his pockets, grinning amiably all the while. The second time around, he sorted through his wallet with careful deliberation, making apologetic but unconvincing 'won't-be-long' noises. The ticket collector leaned patiently against the door-frame. He had often dealt with louts of this sort before.

Triumphantly, Raven produced his travel warrant, a flimsy sheet of official print.

'Count up to one, can you, son?'

Raven feigned innocence mingled with disinterest. He had practised on harder uniforms than this one.

The ticket collector balanced himself against the sway of the carriage as the train raced across a junction. Suspicions confirmed, his voice grew even less pleasant. 'See that number on the window?'

They both inspected the window carefully. Raven nodded soberly.

'That's a "one", that is. Means it's a first-class compartment. Feet off the seat and get out.'

Raven did not move. 'What about me ticket?'

The man almost snarled. 'Second-class. This is a second-class warrant.'

Raven waved another piece of paper at the irate collector. It was an identical warrant. He looked from one to the other, nonplussed.

The boy grinned. 'Got two of them, ain't I?'

The official asked suspiciously, 'Who's this other one for, then?'

'A lady.'

He shook his head. 'Still only second-class. Where is she?'

Raven grinned up at the cheap suitcase on the opposite rack. 'Chopped her into little pieces. She's in me case...'

The collector backed into the corridor, to make room. 'Out. Come on, out!'

The boy picked up his magazine and leafed through it, trying to find his place. 'Listen,' he said, 'two second-class warrants come to more than one first-class, right? Stands to reason. So I reckon you owe me some change.'

A woman passed along the corridor and forced the collector to enter the compartment again. He was frowning at the warrants. 'Ferndown... that where you come from? I've heard of that. That's a Borstal, isn't it?'

'Borstal?' Raven exploded. 'You got to be joking, squire.' He could hardly prevent the laughter. 'One of the oldest public schools in the country, Ferndown.' That barrack. That grey misery of wire and tarmac that converted the imposed silence into a noise inside your head... how could a man as old as this one, willing to wear his life away inside a uniform, pockets full of authority, a cap braided with self-importance, hope to understand the joke.

'You going to come quietly or do you want bother?'

There it was again, the confrontation. The boy stared down at the photo-report of the riots at the United match, the burning stand. 'I want bother,' he said quietly. A police horse lay on its side, kicking... pity, that. Idiots swarmed across the pitch. The referee trapped in the goal-net, trapped by stupidity and abuse.

The collector eyed the boy across the carriage apprehensively, deterred by his balance, his confidence, his quiet aggression. Making up his mind, he warned, 'I'll make sure it's waiting for you, then...'

The compartment door slammed shut and Raven looked out at the gathering day, miserably. The hawk, small, its blue and yellow colouring dulled by speed and distance, flashed low over the embankment, disappeared behind a forestry plantation and lifted again into line above the train, making the boy glad to be free... if only for a time.

*

A plump, middle-aged lady tossed her paperback into the rear seat of her battered old Mini estate as the train drew into the station.

As the carriages came to a hissing halt, the ticket collector and another guard hurried among the few passengers alighting. Only three passengers entered the train and the doors crashed shut behind them as the two railwaymen peered into each compartment, for at first sight the compartment in which Raven had confronted the ticket collector's authority had proved empty.

The rather eccentric-looking lady from the Mini leaned worriedly over the barrier and watched the men inspect the train. The last of the passengers had passed her and left the station.

An angry-looking ticket collector gave up the search and re-entered the train, indicating that the guard should signal the train to depart. As it shuddered into movement, a giggling Raven leaped down from the luggage-rack on which he had been hiding and, suitcase in hand, opened the door of the moving train and slipped athletically onto the platform, slamming the compartment door behind him.

As the guard shouted something unintelligible, Raven waved cheerfully to him, at the same time making a rather rude but thoroughly satisfying sign to the impotently fuming ticket collector who was leaning from a window further along the train.

The train disappeared into the distance and Raven turned and left the station to be greeted by the worried Mini-lady.

'I'm Georgina Young. You must be Raven. Thought

you'd got lost…' She peered past him. 'Where's your Probation Officer? Miss Pettigrew, isn't it?'

Raven tried to stay deadpan. 'She took the wrong turning. Like… went down to Penzance…'

'Nice at this time of year, Penzance. Still, very odd of her…' She led the way out into the station yard.

Rust fell from the underside of the car as she slid back the driver's window and reached inside to release the doorcatch – there was no longer a handle on the outside – and the door swung open rather tipsily on its one goodish hinge. As she heaved her bulk into the complaining wreck, Mrs Young leaned across and opened the passenger door for Raven. He was staring into the sky.

Following his gaze, she let out a snort of interest and grabbed a pair of binoculars from among the mess in the glove compartment.

'Interested in birds?' She focused carefully.

Raven grinned. 'Not that kind.'

The blue and yellow hawk hovered above them.

Mrs Young threw the glasses into the back of the car and fumbled for the starter. 'I'm an ornithologist,' she beamed.

'Terrific.' Raven had been warned at the school and boredom stretched for miles before him.

'My husband's an archaeologist. You know what that is?'

The car spluttered into life. 'Yeah. Digs up old bones and that.'

'Not only old bones. Ancient civilisations. Your history.'

Raven slumped further into the uncomfortable seat. He tried to be polite and to seem interested. 'History, eh? 1066 and stuff?'

She smiled at his effort. 'The site he's working on is a

good deal older than that.' The car weaved erratically out of the yard and onto the main road, narrowly missing an inoffensive pedestrian. As the thin sound of the tinny hooter faded, Mrs Young turned fully to Raven and smiled her sweetest smile. 'You must forgive me. I haven't had the car long.'

The boy reached for the seat belt and clipped himself into place.

The Mini graunched cheerfully up the last hill and out of the trees into rich farmland. From some distance away, Raven could see the strange group of massive rocks that were to play such a significant role in the next few weeks of his life.

Beside the rocks was an area that had all the marks of being a construction site – high wire fencing, temporary buildings, marker pegs and ballast roads. The main building, a Portakabin, seemed to be what they were aiming for.

'I'm afraid that my husband won't be working here much longer, though. The Government are closing the dig down.'

The Government. The uniforms. That lot again.

Mrs Young skidded the heap to a halt. 'They're building something official here. James is trying to stop them and he's got a lot of local support, but he's fighting a losing battle. Er… you may find him a little short-tempered at the moment.'

The cabin was packed with electronic equipment. A bank of television screens relayed pictures of the great cave system below the rock group via a closed-circuit system. Raven was dazzled by the sight.

In front of the screens, sitting in a wheelchair, was a

crusty, impatient, beak-nosed man. He watched intently as a girl in red helmet and overalls lifted something up from the floor of one of the caves.

On other screens, various similarly attired student-helpers worked, while construction workers passed to and fro. Raven noticed that construction workers were wearing the yellow gear, archaeological workers, red. Each group was readily identifiable and seemed to prefer it that way, to judge by the way they avoided each other.

'Careful. Gently, you stupid girl, I want it in one piece.'

The girl displayed the small stone relic as close to camera as she could manage.

The wheelchair man leaned forward. 'A Cornish cross? What's that doing all the way up here? Turn it around.'

The girl displayed the carved stone. A fish, a snake and two interlocking spirals.

'Probably pre-Christian. Now you moronic female, do you think you could manage to bring it up without damaging it?'

The girl grinned and moved out of shot. The wheelchair spun suddenly and Raven found himself staring into the most piercing gaze he had ever encountered.

Mrs Young broke the silence. 'James, this is Raven.'

The eyes bored into the boy. 'Raven?'

Raven smiled wearily; he had met this type of attack before. He held the gaze as he slowly shook his head. 'It's a long story…'

The eyes snapped off. 'Well, don't bore me with it now. I'm busy.' The wheelchair spun sharply.

Mrs Young's no-nonsense voice cut across the rudeness. 'Now James, you promised you'd give the boy a chance…'

There was a pause. A moment. The man's voice softened slightly. 'Georgina, I want to take a look at that cross. Wheel me to the lift, will you, my dear?'

Raven cleared the doorway and again found himself staring into those eyes. The voice hardened again. 'Stay here. Watch, listen – but don't touch.'

Before he could stop himself, Raven's training made him straighten up and say, 'Yes, sir.'

'I want to make one thing quite clear,' he heard through his resentment. 'It wasn't my idea to have you to stay. If I'd had my way, you'd still be in the Home, serving out your sentence.'

The voice droned on. The reasonable, practical argument that had been thrown at him by all the 'straights' he had ever met. What was that bit in the Bible about casting the first stone? But then, who reads the Bible and applies the lessons to his own existence, nowadays? The Chaplain was always the first to fill the ear with wisdom and good advice but that did not stop him from being the worst gossip in the town and the first to accuse others in the Home of any discovered faults, however minor.

'My wife, who is a little soft in the head, persuaded me to welcome you. The slightest breach of discipline, however, and you go straight back where you came from. Understood?'

Raven left it the regulation insulting pause before he muttered, 'Understood.'

'Good. Now wait here until we get back. And keep your hands off those controls.'

Mrs Young manoeuvred the chair through the narrow doorway and down the ramp, but before she disappeared she turned and gave Raven an encouraging wink. The boy was surprised. Mrs Young did not look like the sort of woman who winked a great deal. Despite his growing resentment at the old man's attitude, he found himself grinning back at her.

Raven turned and considered the closed-circuit television system. Fascinating toy… he could quite see why the old man wanted to keep it all to himself. On each screen of the monitor bank something was happening – construction workers and archaeology students trying, not too successfully in some cases, to carry out their very different work side by side. In one cave there was a shouting match going on, a student getting a right stripping from an official-looking yellow hat. Just as it was getting really interesting, the cabin door opened and a man stopped in the doorway, surprised to find the boy at the tele-desk.

'Hello… can I help you?' He sounded as though he doubted it.

Muscular, a likeable, open face and an honest, capable manner impressed Raven on first sight. This was the only fellow he had met so far who looked as though he might be worth knowing… an obvious mate. Certainly looked as though he knew how to take care of himself.

'I'm with the Youngs.' Raven suddenly grinned.

The doubt disappeared and the fellow grinned back. He threw his yellow helmet on the top of a filing cabinet and moved to the desk at the far end of the cabin. 'I don't envy you. I have to share this office with him, so I know what he's like to live with.'

'Always like that, is he?' Raven still did not know quite what to call the old grouch.

'The Professor?' The construction man shook his head patiently. 'Ever since we arrived he's been giving us a hard time... he's so defensive about his precious caves.'

Raven waited but the paperwork had started. The fellow seemed to have forgotten that he was standing there. The boy moved to the desk which was littered with charts and half-covered with a scale model of the area. The great standing stones were easy to pick out. 'What are you doing here? What are you doing in the caves?'

A calloused finger stabbed at the part of the model that showed what appeared to be a Martian factory, all connected buildings, of some far-advanced design.

The boy studied it. 'Looks like a load of plastic crockery stuck together with spaghetti.'

'It's a nuclear waste reprocessing plant. We're using the caves to store the garbage. Correction. We will be doing so – that's the plan. And your friend doesn't like it.'

Raven ran his fingers over the model; it was curiously beautiful, the white curvature of the buildings, the complexity of the pipe-work. 'Couldn't you go somewhere else? What's so special about this place?'

The man at the desk looked up at him quizzically. 'The surveyors say these caves are the ideal place to store the stuff after it's been treated, so the Professor has only a month left to finish his work. Then he and his long-haired weirdos have to leave.'

Raven glanced at the screens and began to understand the tensions between the rival groups of workers. 'Why are the caves so important to the... the Professor?'

The fellow became more guarded. If the boy was with the Professor, why was he asking such naive questions? And so openly? He frowned. 'Don't ask me. All I know is the silly old buffer holds me responsible. As if it were my decision.'

'The old lady said he was still trying to stop you.'

Papers shuffled across the desk. 'He can try. But he won't get anywhere... you can't stop progress, can you?'

Raven agreed there. 'Silly to try, nowadays. Still, this nuclear stuff that you're burying...?'

'Plutonium waste.'

'Yeah.' Raven searched through his recent memory. Surely he had read something somewhere on that. 'That's dangerous, innit?'

The man went to the filing cabinet. 'Stays dangerous for a quarter of a million years. So if you don't stick it somewhere safe, you're in trouble.'

Seemed reasonable. Confident that the fellow knew what he was talking about, Raven felt even more that there were problems to come in his new home life. 'No good living in the past. Got to look after the future, right?'

'Right.' The great horny hand was stuck under the boy's nose. Raven took it and his arm was pumped up and down forcefully. 'My name's Bill... Bill Telford. We'll probably be seeing quite a bit of each other these next few weeks.'

Raven was pleased. He felt, somehow, that he and Bill Telford were going to be friends.

*

The house proved to be a large, crumbling rectory standing in its own grounds, at the end of a narrow lane.

Raven's room was at the head of the staircase. It was small, and had probably been a servant's room when the

13

house was in its prime. Mrs Young sat on the end of the bed, watching Raven unpack. As the boy pinned a poster to the wall, she caught sight of a framed photograph of a bird in his case.

Raven reached into the grip and waved the photograph at Mrs Young. 'It's a picture of me Dad.'

Mrs Young stared at the picture incredulously. '*Corvus corax*,' she said.

The boy laughed nervously. 'Sounds like a disease.'

It was a photograph of a large glossy black raven...

'*Corvus corax* is Latin for raven.' Mrs Young sounded worried.

'Better not tell the others at the Home.' Raven placed the picture on his bedside table. 'Just imagine: oi, you – *Corvus corax*, come here! They'd send me up, rotten.'

Mrs Young looked interested. 'Tell me about it?' she asked.

'What, me Dad?' Raven grinned. 'I was a foundling, see. Found, as a baby, right in the middle of... here, I've got a postcard...' He rummaged around in his case and came up with another picture. 'Right in the middle of that.'

Mrs Young stared at the photograph of the earthwork maze at the top of the hill.

'Right? There was this bird standing next to me – the farmer said it looked like it was on guard. Wouldn't leave me side until it knew I was safe – that's how I got me name.'

'And you never traced your parents?'

'No.' There was a brief silence. 'The orphanage made a few enquiries but nobody wanted to know... except dear old Dad, here – he cared.' Raven gazed at the picture of the great black bird with something approaching respect.

'Didn't you, Dad? The only one…'

Mrs Young regarded the boy carefully. It was difficult to know when he was being serious. There was obviously a good mind hidden beneath that shock of hair, behind that flippant, aggressive exterior. 'Is that how you became interested in birds?'

Up went that rather scathing barrier. 'Who says I'm interested in birds?'

Mrs Young was stung into reply. 'You were interested in one today. At the station.'

'Oh, that.' The dismissive shrug. 'I saw it from the train. Followed us for miles, it did. Stopped when I got out. Just hung there in the sky.'

*

Supper was eaten in the big kitchen. Apart from the normal cupboards and shelves of preserves and goodies the kitchen walls were crowded with Mrs Young's collection of stuffed birds in glass cases. There was something almost eerie about glancing up from one's food to stare into several hungry beaked faces. Raven decided that the silence was too much and he started enjoying his food rather noisily. Professor Young picked at his plate and conned the large-scale cave chart that spread itself over most of the table. While Mrs Young was at the Aga, the telephone rang.

Raven answered it, as he was nearest and the others seemed busy. The operator asked if he would like to pay for a reverse-charge call from Cornwall. Raven was on the point of refusing when Mrs Young took the receiver from him and accepted the call. It was Miss Pettigrew, the Probation Officer whose rail warrant he had offered to the ticket collector on the train. By the look on Mrs Young's face and the shrill squawks issuing from the receiver, Miss Pettigrew was not pleased at finding herself so far from home.

Mrs Young replaced the receiver and shook her head sadly at Raven. 'I don't think she's too amused.'

'Really? Tough.'

'I don't think she wanted to go to Penzance. She doesn't have her fare back.'

'Shame.' Raven shrugged it off. The uniforms could look after themselves. 'People should always carry extra bread. In case of these emergencies, like…'

The cheese was passed to the Professor but he shook his head and continued to be absorbed in the chart. Mrs Young went to busy herself with coffee. 'There are some emergencies that it would be impossible to anticipate,' she said, drily.

Raven tried to read the chart, upside down. 'Plan of the caves?' The old man ignored him. Raven took an apple and bit deep into it. 'Talking to Bill Telford,' he mumbled through the juices. 'Says you've got to be out of there in a month.'

The Professor raised his eyes, irked by the boy's confident tone. 'That remains to be seen.'

'Thought it was all settled.'

'It is *not* all settled.' He folded the chart, disliking the defensive feeling that the boy was engendering in him. 'The Minister is coming down in a few weeks to hear our Appeal. We hope to make him see sense.'

Raven grinned. He could see he had nettled the old chap. 'Bill don't think you've got a prayer…'

'Naturally. If we succeed, he's out of a job.'

That did not sound likely. A man of Telford's ability would find a new job immediately. Why was the old boy so touchy? Why couldn't he discuss the subject coolly and calmly? It was obviously a very emotional approach that he had to the problem. Raven wickedly decided to keep riding him, to see how far he could go before he got the Professor's goat entirely. 'What about this nuclear waste, then? Got to put it somewhere, right?'

'Wrong!'

Raven had done it. In one. The Professor's eye gleamed bright and his face started purpling. He was obviously holding himself in check with difficulty. The boy grinned happily at his discomfiture.

'Wrong. There are plenty of other sources of power. All they're doing is exposing future generations to the danger of radioactive contamination, and vandalising the countryside in the process.'

The lecture had started. Raven cut across it quickly. 'Got to move with the times, Prof. Can I have the cheese back? This is the twentieth century, not the Dark Ages.'

The Professor climbed to the summit of his anger. 'What do you know about it? An illiterate lout from Borstal?'

His wife tried to keep the peace. 'James… he's just trying to understand.'

The Professor fumed. He stared at the boy with something approaching contempt. 'People like that will never understand.'

Raven was enjoying himself. After all, he did not really care one way or another what happened to a load of industrial garbage. But he did like climbing up authority's nose and in this situation the Professor was very much the representative of the uniformed brigade. Raven decided to lead on. 'How about giving me a chance? I mean what's so special about your bunch of holes in the ground?' That was surely an offer the old man would not refuse.

He didn't. He rose to the bait. 'It's special because the system is thousands of years old. Because it was a sacred area.'

'Sacred?' That was something Bill had not mentioned. 'Sort of underground church, like?'

'Precisely.' The Professor had noticed the moment of interest from the boy and pressed his small advantage with missionary fervour. 'All the indications are that the caves are man-made, hewn out of the rock by ancient priests, perhaps to serve as a place of refuge from invaders... Romans... others... My interest is not in the cave-builders but in those who used the system some five centuries later... and the man who led them.'

Raven stared at the old man and waited for him to go on but the Professor needed a response and waited too. Eye to eye, they tried each other. Raven knew the tactic but in that knowledge he also knew that he was confident enough to play the game well. 'So. Who was their leader?'

The Professor, not sure of Raven's next move, waited a moment longer. 'Arthur.'

The boy put on his innocent face. 'Arthur who, Guv?'

'Arthur the King. King Arthur. Even you must have heard of...'

'Oh, him... his bird ran off with his best mate, right?'

The Professor sipped at his coffee. It was disgusting.

'Crudely put, but basically accurate.'

Raven sucked the sugar from the end of his coffee spoon. 'Local boy, was he?'

'Legends of Arthur abound in this part of the country. Most of the relics we have found so far tend to support the theory.'

Mrs Young pointed to a jar on the top of a cupboard. 'Like that earthenware vase. Splendid... that's fifth century, more or less.'

The Professor looked up at the perfectly ordinary-looking bit of pottery. 'One can't be too precise but it was certainly made about the time Arthur was supposed to have existed.'

Despite himself, Raven could feel his interest growing; now that the conversation was about a personality, the idea had become less generalised, more – well, history ought to be about people, not just about their bones. 'Supposed to? You mean there never was such a bloke?'

'I doubt it.' The Professor sounded certain enough. 'Some people believe that Arthur was the name of the office, rather than of a particular person. Derived from the Celtic word *Ariwane*... meaning "Chief of the Bear Folk".'

That was more like it. 'Chief, eh?'

'Probably a succession of them. Leaders who rose up to defend the kingdom whenever it was in danger.'

So those ancient tribes had the same problems as today. 'Commanders, like... hard men, who just took command...?'

The Professor looked at the boy curiously. Something passed between them: neither of them knew what the feeling was but they were both aware of its arrival. 'That's right.'

Raven felt something stir inside him, some memory that he could not place, a feeling that brought him for some stupid reason close to tears. It was eerie… he had not cried for years, since he was a kid. He swallowed hard. 'These blokes… how would they know they were Arthur?'

The Professor shrugged. The moment had passed; they were back to needling, back to the silly, inconsequential questions, were they? 'I've no idea. Perhaps they received some sort of sign.'

*

Above the house, hanging against the evening sky, the blue and yellow bird was touched by the last rays of the dying sun…

Chapter Two

RAVEN CLATTERED THROUGH THE GATEWAY of the construction site on Mrs Young's bicycle which had already seen its best years before the coming of the Mini; twice the chain had come off when freewheeling downhill and the saddle was doing uncomfortable and unnecessary damage minute by minute. The boy weaved his way through a bunch of workmen and fell off the wreck as he reached the Portakabin – it seemed to be the only obvious way to stop the beast as neither brake worked. The local Road Safety office ought to have a sledgehammer that people could borrow to put such animals out of their misery.

Bill Telford was working at his desk as Raven stuck his head in through the cabin door. 'Hullo, mate. Where's the Prof?'

'Said he had work to do. Told me to get lost.' Raven grinned at Telford, nodding towards the monitor bank. 'Can't get *Match of the Day* on that lot, can you?'

'Too exciting. Might blow a fuse.' Telford did something complicated with a slide-rule.

Raven waited for him to finish. 'I was wondering… any chance of me getting down in the caves, have a look-see?'

The construction boss shook his head. 'Got a pass? The Professor give you one, did he?'

Raven shifted uncomfortably; this was not the reaction he had expected from Bill. It smacked of officialdom – a pass to see some grotty old grottoes. 'I didn't tell him where I was going.'

'Can't let you wander around on your tod. It's against regulations.' There, he'd said it. Very disappointing attitude from a mate.

'Yeah, yeah… regulations.' Another uniformed mind.

Telford saw the boy's disappointment and thought it was to do with not being allowed down the cave shaft. He did not yet know enough about Raven's spirit and the way it rebelled against imposed disciplines that seemed to the boy in any way unnecessary or unjust. 'Tell you what, I'm supposed to be taking someone else down this morning. Come with us.'

There was a knock at the door of the cabin. Raven moved to open it.

'Mr Telford?'

An attractive girl stood outside on the ramp. Eighteen years old, blonde and vivacious, she seemed uncertain but at the same time oddly composed. Very much her own woman – very together.

It was Raven who suddenly felt all knees and elbows – those eyes definitely had something. 'Won't I do?' he tried.

'Is Mr Telford in?' She was insistent.

Raven stood aside and the girl brushed past – which did not improve his peace of mind. She really was very beautiful, he decided.

'I'm from the *Midshires Herald*, I believe you're expecting me?' Now it was Bill's turn to get the treatment and it seemed to be affecting him in just about the same way.

'They told me that they were sending a man.' He sounded unsure. 'Name of Grant.'

A ripple of laughter made Raven suddenly feel how grubby and ramshackle his surroundings were. He had not been aware of the shabbiness of the cabin furnishings until this moment. The girl smiled at them both. 'Naomi Grant. That's me. I hope you're not too disappointed?'

They were neither of them disappointed at all.

Telford was the first to recover. 'This is Raven. He's coming down with us.'

Naomi blessed the boy with her best smile and it was good. He had not been on the receiving end of many smiles like that. 'Raven?' she enquired as she offered her hand.

'Raven,' he said as he took her hand, hesitantly. He hated her, really, for making him feel like some awkward twelve year old.

But then she said, 'Naomi,' and he felt himself grow sure and certain that he had met a friend.

*

Bill led them across the site towards an overhang of rock. Raven was surprised to see the hidden shaft disappearing into the rockface. The tunnel was brightly lit and they stumbled along to the top of the lift shaft in single file, Bill first, with Raven bringing up the rear.

The lift cage was large, modern and obviously very newly installed. Alongside the cage area was a series of lockers and equipment hanging on hooks driven into the rock. Bill started sorting among the spare gear that was there.

'You'll need a pair of overalls and a helmet.'

Raven liked the thought of getting into the yellow overalls that Bill offered him, and as he struggled into them he noticed a small device sewn into the denim just over the breast pocket. 'What's this thing?'

Bill zipped himself into a suit. 'It's a telltale. Registers the presence of gas. Starts turning red. When there's no green left, you're in trouble. Are you OK, Miss Grant?'

They turned to see how she was getting on and found that she was even more fetching in overalls than before, if that were possible.

'Sorry about the gear,' said Bill, 'it's a company rule.' And he led the way into the lift cage, slamming the doorgate shut when they were all inside.

The descent was slow and quiet. Bill started on the details immediately. 'We want all the publicity we can get, Miss Grant. So far the Prof's lot have made all the noise – carrying on about our national heritage and that. But nobody's put the other side of the argument... Nobody's talked about the advantages of a place like this, explained how nuclear waste can be stored here for ever in complete safety.'

Naomi froze him with a flash of those eyes. 'Don't worry, Mr Telford. My editor's on your side.'

Bill immediately dropped the charm and his natural aggression slipped back into place. 'Sounds as if you aren't,'

24

he said quietly.

Naomi realised that she had made her point and grinned at Raven rather wickedly. 'I'm just a junior reporter. I do as I'm told.'

The cage reached the bottom of the shaft and the gate crashed open. Raven and Naomi stared about them, fascinated. They were in a large cave from which two other caves led off, on either side of a thick pillar of rock. Above the entrance to each of the caves was a symbol carved into the rock... The whole complex was brilliantly lit and, glancing about him, Raven soon spotted the television camera for this cave that connected with one of the monitors in the Portakabin. The whole area was busy with both construction workers and archaeology students.

Raven fastened his helmet. 'What's that, then?' he asked, staring up at one of the symbols over the cave entrance.

Naomi chanced, 'Looks like a unicorn.'

'There's a carving outside each of the caves... all different,' explained Bill. 'There's another one over there.'

'A giant.' Naomi frowned, trying to see the meaning.

'Marvellous, innit?' Raven avoided a group of workers. 'In them days you could carve what you liked on the walls. Now you get nicked for it.'

Bill led them through into another cave. Above the entrance was carved yet another symbol which Naomi volunteered was a rather crude representation of a ship.

'Reckon they're religious?' asked Raven. 'The Prof reckons this place had something to do with religion.'

Bill snapped back, contemptuously. 'He's just guessing. You know what these cranks are – pull down a pile of rubble in the middle of nowhere and they tell you you're destroying some ancient architect's masterpiece.'

*

The ship symbol flicked onto the screen that had been set up in the dark, book-lined room. Despite the fact that the windows were open, the room was haunted with shadows, even in daylight. Stuffed birds in cases vied for position around the room with labelled stone relics of various shapes and sizes.

The Professor sat in his wheelchair before the screen, operating a small slide-projector. He pressed a button and another slide appeared before him – a primitive carving of a girl.

*

Raven and the others stared up at the carving of the girl over the cave entrance. The boy grinned at Naomi. 'My favourite, that. Dunno why.'

Bill continued with his 'suitability argument', as he called it – trying to impress on Naomi the necessity for storing nuclear waste in this cave system. 'Our geologists say this is the most stable area in the country. No danger of earth tremors or anything like that. And the rock forms a natural barrier against any possible leakage of radiation… we've tried dumping nuclear waste at sea but the water started corroding the concrete shielding.'

Naomi turned unexpectedly to Raven. She measured him carefully with, 'What do you think?'

Raven, on the hop, only managed, 'Me?'

'We're going to have to live with a time-bomb under our feet. Doesn't that worry you?' Naomi waited.

The boy shrugged and tried to turn away. 'Nothing to do with me.'

'You don't think we should try to stop it?'

She was becoming a nuisance. 'Look, if Bill says it's safe, it's safe.'

Naomi put that to one side. 'He's committed to the project, aren't you, Mr Telford?'

Raven leaped in, getting angry. 'I'll take his word for it. He's my mate. And he's the expert.'

'Something tells me I'm not getting through to you, Miss Grant.' Bill tried to calm the moment.

'It's not me you have to convince, Mr Telford – I'm bound by the editorial policy of my paper. But you seem to be getting through to people like him, all right.' She withered Raven with her gorgeous eyes. 'And if the younger generation isn't prepared to stand up and fight, then there's nothing to stop you, is there?' She turned and stalked away into the next cave. Bill and Raven stared after her in astonishment.

*

The symbol on the screen showed a carving of a sitting bird with its head twisted around from its body to look behind it. On its head was a primitive representation of a star. The Professor sat motionless staring at the slide until the door opened and Mrs Young bustled in.

'You rang, dear?'

The Professor nodded at the screen. 'What do you make of that fellow?'

Mrs Young peered closely at the screen. 'Could be anything. No legs, so it's symbolically nesting... a plover, perhaps?'

The Professor's eyes lit up at that. 'Interesting...' He grabbed a thick volume from the desk. 'Listen to this.' He found the page that he was looking for. 'This mythical bird, supposed by some to be a kind of plover, is often depicted with human arms. Others consider it to be sacred to the Egyptian god Osiris and it is sometimes represented with a star upon the head.'

Mrs Young took the book from him. 'What mythical bird?'

'The phoenix.'

She replaced the great tome on the desk. 'Supposed to rise from the ashes of its funeral pyre.'

'Exactly. The symbol of rebirth.'

They were both aware that they were stumbling about in an area of almost total darkness, well outside both their specialised fields.

Mrs Young changed direction. 'How many symbols are there, down in the caves?'

The Professor tried to follow her. 'Eleven. Eleven caves. Eleven symbols... but this one seems more important than the rest. It's twice the size of the others.'

His wife continued gnawing at the problem he had set. 'Rebirth? Did the Arthurians believe in reincarnation?'

'Maybe it refers to the caves. Let's hope it's a sign that the place itself is indestructible.'

*

Telford stopped and looked at a group of artifacts piled against the cave wall. A girl student was noting the sizes of the most interesting. 'Look at that...' Bill sneered. 'They're appealing to the Minister to kill this project – and for what? A few bits of old stone.'

He led the way towards the lift shaft, his tour of the system completed. 'That's the trouble with this country. Anyone tries to build a bypass so traffic can move a bit faster or suggests putting a reservoir within a hundred miles of a beauty spot, and there's always some crackpot ready to start up a national campaign against it.'

Raven grinned as he saw how badly Naomi was taking this. Just to rub it in, he volunteered, 'That's why we're in a mess… because of people like the Prof.'

They entered the lift cage as Telford continued. 'I'll tell you something, mate. The only reason tourists come to Britain is to have a good laugh. It's like a doll's house compared with the rest of the world – a doll's house with no mod cons.'

*

High above the Youngs' house, the small blue and yellow hawk circled, effortlessly riding a thermal, watching, waiting for its moment.

Raven clanked along the lane. It had been quite a morning. As he came out of the trees, the bank fell away, giving him a clear view across the fields to the big old house, nestling among its outbuildings. It had a friendly feel to it, the house. It was a house of families… a home in the most proper sense. It smiled down the lane at him.

The bird stopped its circling and hung motionless in the noon sky. Raven saw it and it caused him to wobble to a halt, the better to watch it. It hung, unbelievably still in the hot air, its wingtips fingering the blue haze of the day.

The Professor was working at his desk in the bay window of his study. He looked up as he saw Raven turn in at the gate and speed up the curve of the drive.

The bird swooped low past Raven and, like an arrow, hurled itself towards the open window of the Professor's study. It alighted gracefully on the sill and hopped into the room.

Raven hurled the bike to the gravel and tried to stare into the room but it was dark from the glare of the sun on the glass and the outside walls. He could see that the Professor was at his desk; the bird was perched on his arm. He started to run towards the house, towards the window, hurdling flowerbeds, tearing across the lawns.

The bird held the Professor's arm firmly as it perched, its beak close to his face. Its behaviour was quite unlike anything the Professor had experienced in a wild bird. It was so sure, so certain. He stared into its unwinking eye, puzzled... the bird regarded him with what seemed almost an affectionate gaze. Suddenly the Professor felt himself begin to relax, the bird's eye was somehow bright and full of... wisdom... Moments later, the bird set its head quizzically on one side and the Professor began, slowly, to smile...

When Raven arrived, breathless, at the window, the room was empty. Even allowing for the darkness inside the room as his eyes accustomed themselves to the gloom, he could see that there was no Professor and definitely no bird. No live bird, that was. The whole room was crowded, in the few spaces between books, with the glass cases which contained Mrs Young's ornithological specimens – but none of them stirred, none of them looked back at the puzzled boy.

He dashed along the front of the house and through its cool hallway to the door of the Professor's study... it was locked. Raven was completely at a loss. He had not daydreamed the entire event? The bird had passed so close to him as it stooped and swooped past the bicycle that he had felt the breath of its wings on his cheek. He searched through the kitchen, the outhouses. He called through the house, but there was no answer. The Mini was gone, Mrs Young was gone, the Professor was nowhere to be seen. The house was deserted, apart from himself. Suddenly a chill crept into the sunlight.

*

Raven lay in bed, reading a gun magazine. His small room he already thought of as a haven. He glanced around at his few possessions. They all seemed so normal and that cheered him. Quite unlike some of the gloomy corners of this old house, the room was easy and had a contented atmosphere. That business of the bird still worried him. Mrs Young had been no great help. She had been in town, shopping. The Professor had not appeared for supper and Raven's attempt to explain the curious events of the afternoon met with blank incredulity from the dizzy lady birdwatcher who told him that quite obviously he had a touch of the sun and had imagined the whole thing. It was most unlikely that any hawk would behave in such a manner. Raven was close to believing her, as it all seemed a very unlikely story, these few hours later.

There was a knock on the door and Mrs Young, in voluminous nightdress and a hairnet, poked her head into the room. Raven, reacting with instinctive Borstal reflex, sprang out of bed and stood to attention in his pyjamas. As he did it, he felt stupid. That was the effect of imposed discipline... brainwashing... it stopped you thinking, stopped you developing a discipline of your own, one that would see you through every circumstance, not just those to which you were geared. He relaxed, feeling foolish.

Mrs Young closed the door behind her. 'I was wondering if you remembered what you did with your knife and fork after supper? I can't seem to find them.'

Raven felt himself turn red. Damn the training, it tore apart his inner niceties at every turn. He reached for his jacket, wordlessly took the cutlery from the breast pocket and handed the pieces to his foster-mother.

She frowned, wondering... 'You wouldn't have got much of a price for them, you know. They are not at all valuable.'

The explanation. Raven shook his head at its naivety. 'I wasn't going to flog them... honest.'

Mrs Young waited but it was difficult for the boy. He did not want to make excuses for his behaviour so soon in his stay, but she obviously thought he was a petty thief. Quietly, he said, 'It's what we have to do at the Home. Wash the tools and keep them until the next meal.' The embarrassment was worse than he thought possible. Now she would start feeling sorry for him.

Her expression cleared and then softened in sympathy. He was right.

'All those years behind bars. And what has it taught you?'

Raven tightened. Attack. Who needs patronising like

this? 'Not to get caught.' He laughed icily.

Mrs Young was not to be shaken off so easily. 'Nothing else?'

Shock her. 'How to pick locks. Disconnect alarms. Stuff like that.' If the truth be known, this was not helping. He was beginning to feel even more childish.

'I believe you're aware of a more important lesson. Miss Pettigrew told me she had high hopes for you – that you'd soon be a credit to any society.'

'Pettigrew's a nut.'

Mrs Young watched his embarrassment grow. For all the bravado, the boy was not yet a man. 'When I asked her who would be most likely to benefit from a month with us, she had no hesitation in suggesting you.'

Raven grinned back at her. 'That's because she fancies me...'

The grin was infectious. Mrs Young responded, drily, 'That's why she went down to Penzance was it? Because of her unrequited love for you?'

They both giggled suddenly – the conversation was becoming daft. 'Right. She's just trying to forget me...'

Mrs Young sobered for a moment. 'There's one thing you mustn't forget, Raven. You're on trial here. You have a golden chance to prove to the authorities that you are capable of behaving yourself without supervision. Don't let us down, will you? There's a lot my husband and I can teach you, if you're willing to learn.'

'Two questions,' he interrupted. 'Where is the Prof, why didn't he eat with us?'

Mrs Young waited. 'What's the other question?'

'That bird. The one that did fly in the study window...

the one we saw at the station… what type is it? What sort?'

She paused at the door, thoughtfully. 'Its Latin name is *Falco aesalon*. It nests on the ground, often among large stones… which is why it's known as the stone falcon.'

Raven found himself staring at the framed photograph of the raven at his bedside. He looked up as the door closed on Mrs Young's quiet 'Goodnight.' Puzzled, he said, 'Stone falcon… Ask him what he's following me around for, will you, Dad?'

*

Hours later, the whole house creaked in its sleep as Raven silently slipped out of his room.

There were two ways of traversing a staircase late at night, in order not to wake a snoring household… either to keep as close to the wall as possible on each tread – that way sudden squeaks and noises from the old timbers were minimised – or, more amusingly and more quickly, to slide silently down the banister. Raven swished down fast and dropped to the polished parquet. He had not even heard himself but all his training made him wait for a reaction. None came.

The study door was still locked. In total darkness, Raven fashioned a short piece of wire into a simple shape. Moments later the old, well-oiled lock slipped silently back into its open position and the door swung ajar… who said the Home had taught him nothing? Copybook stuff. Ten out of ten, so far.

Inside the room, he moved as fast as darkness would allow. The door locked again with the bent wire 'key', he crossed the room to the window and drew the curtains quite shut. Only then did he flash the thin bright beam of his pencil torch across the spines of the books on the shelves.

It took him some minutes to find the book he was looking for – *Birds of the British Isles*. He took the great illustrated tome and turned to the index.

Leafing through the pages he came to the one he wanted… the blue and yellow hawk. *Falco aesalon*. The stone falcon. His torch beam picked out the bird's beady eyes and the beauty of the plumage.

As the torch flickered through the text alongside, Raven felt something stir within him… some unnameable feeling… He had known all along, without knowing… *Falco aesalon*. The stone falcon. More commonly known as a merlin…

Chapter Three

RAVEN WAS DISTURBED. WHY SHOULD such feelings be aroused in his mind by a bird? It had followed him here, it had entered the house, it had some strange meaning that he was unable to fathom.

From the passage outside came the sound of a birdlike squealing, a fluttering. A key turned in the lock of the door and it slowly swung open. The curtains moved as though some unseen force had entered the room. Raven froze to the spot as the book slipped from his fingers. Outside, on the wall of the hallway, he saw the shadow of a huge beaked creature. Cold sweat broke out on his body as his fear turned to panic.

Suddenly Raven let out a hoarse cry of laughter for the shadow had resolved itself in the doorway – it was the Professor, seated in his wheelchair. The squeals were the sound of the rubber tyres on the parquet, the flutterings were the Professor's still uncompleted attempt to get into his dressing gown while in his wheelchair!

But was this the Professor? His beakiness was more pronounced than ever – but there was also something else... He looked down at Raven's feet, where the book lay open and the picture of the merlin stared up at them both.

Through Raven's mind raced the events of the afternoon. The bird swooping low past him and disappearing into the study, where, he was certain, the old man had been working at the desk in the window. The bird had hopped inside onto the desk, onto the Professor's arm... but then what? What had happened to the bird? What had happened to the Professor?

Raven looked up to find the Professor's eyes twinkling at him. The grumpy old curmudgeon had gone, and in his place sat a kindly, beaming friend.

Raven waited for some unkind change to take place. Waited for the rucking for being in the man's study in the middle of the night, and the demand for an explanation. When it came he was really surprised. In a soft and gentle half-whisper, the Professor asked, 'Hello, old lad. Can I help you find whatever it is you are looking for...?' He wheeled himself out of the shadows and switched on a reading light at the desk – a light which cast even stranger shadows in the room.

Suddenly Mrs Young appeared in the doorway holding a twelve-bore shotgun at arm's length. The Professor positively giggled. 'Put that away, my dear. It's only our boy.' He grinned at Raven, 'Don't worry, it isn't loaded.'

His wife looked relieved and sheepish, all bravado gone. 'We've never had any cartridges. Too dangerous.' The Professor gently took the gun from her and laid it in his lap, as Mrs Young said, apologetically, 'I thought it was burglars...'

The old man laughed and caught Raven's eye conspiratorially. 'Don't suppose we'd have heard anything if you'd been burgling would we...?'

Raven shook his head. What a pair! The Professor and Mrs Young smiled. Raven found, to his surprise, that he was grinning back. It was a ridiculous situation and he had completely lost track of what the expected attitudes should be.

For the others they were feeling that contact with the boy was slowly being established. At Raven's pace...

The Professor spun the chair into the hall and past the staircase. Raven followed. 'I'd better lock this away,' said the Professor. 'Goodnight, Raven.' He and the boy held the look for a moment but the intimacy was too much for Raven. He broke away and started up the stairs.

Turning, he nodded scathingly at the gun. 'Just a toy, that thing.'

The Professor examined the gun and looked up at the boy. 'It has its uses.'

'Not much use without cartridges.'

Mrs Young came out into the hallway. 'It's just for show, Raven. This is a lonely spot. All we need is something to – to bluff with. Frighten off intruders...'

The boy laughed. 'You want to frighten people? Chop eight, nine inches off the barrel.'

There was a pause as the couple worked this out. 'A sawn-off shotgun...?' The Professor sounded intrigued but worried. 'That's illegal, isn't it?'

Raven grinned. 'Very. Also very effective. You don't

want to mess with shooters unless you know what you're doing.'

The significance of his remark hung like a question mark between them. Mrs Young just had to ask... 'You've had experience with – er – shooters?'

'No.' The boy half turned away. 'I just know they go bang. And only mugs use them. But any pro could tell that was an antique. Take my advice, sell it – buy a dog.'

He was gone, up the stairs, two at a time, suddenly shy of the intimacy that was growing between them. The Professor and Mrs Young watched him until his bedroom door closed.

The Professor glanced again at the gun. 'That sounded like professional advice, my dear.'

Mrs Young wheeled him towards his ground-floor bedroom. 'Remarkable young man...'

'Indeed.' The Professor smiled fondly up at her. 'You chose well.'

*

Raven sat on the edge of his bed, staring at his framed picture of the old raven. 'Know something, old feller?' he whispered, 'I reckon I'm going bananas. For a moment there, I thought the old Prof was... well, you wouldn't believe it...'

*

The Professor placed a domed-glass case on his desk and turned it until its contents were staring back at him... the beady eyes of the stuffed merlin, proud in its setting of fern and rock.

*

In the darkness of the small bedroom, the boy turned quickly in his sleep. Somewhere in the room there was the strong fluttering of wings, the sound penetrating even into the depths of sleep... Raven's eyelids flickered open as he lay listening, half awake. Then sleep stole back with the silence. The curtains moved. Outside was the quiet of the world at night.

*

The merlin was brought up the stairs. Mrs Young's hand clasped the glass-domed case carefully to her ample bosom as, with her free hand, she carried a steaming cup of morning coffee.

The Professor was sitting at his desk in the study. As his wife climbed the stairs, his whole being seemed concentrated on her journey. He listened and his breath was shallow, almost stopped, as he travelled with her without moving...

*

Raven was under the bedclothes as the dim light from the half-open door behind the glass-domed case on the bedside table revealed the merlin in silhouette. The curtains swished open and Raven sat bolt upright in bed. Mrs Young looked dark against the sun, as his eyes struggled against the harsh morning light. A steaming coffee mug was set down before the glass case and, as Raven blinked his way towards the delicious aroma of it, the bird seemed to move through the steam, seemed almost to be living in the heat-shimmer.

He heard Mrs Young's voice through the haze of

morning consciousness. 'It's a *Falco aesalon* – the bird you were so interested in – or rather the one you thought was so interested in you. I didn't realise we had a specimen. He's yours if you want him.' She was somewhere by the door, now. 'Breakfast's ready…' Raven looked up at her over the rim of the mug, the coffee-smell luxuriating in his nostrils. 'Rare in this part of the country,' she wittered on in her kindly way, 'very rare. Plenty of hawks and falcons around here but never a merlin. I'll write to *The Times*…' And she was gone, leaving the boy staring at the bird.

*

Raven slid down the banister, repeating his midnight performance, but this time just practising. As he reached the newel post and slid to the parquet he looked up to see the Professor watching his antics from the study.

'Good morning.' The Professor's smile was tolerant, condescending. He obviously thought Raven was doing something childish, and Raven scowled, half-embarrassed. If only the old man knew.

The smile stayed quite genuine. What had happened to the old curmudgeon of yesterday? The crusty, fussy, pedant had become friendly and fatherly overnight. Raven wondered whether the Professor would demand an explanation for his behaviour the night before. It was strange. At the time it almost seemed as if he already knew the answers and did not need to ask the obvious questions. Raven hesitated in the study doorway.

'Come in, come in…' The Professor indicated a pile of books. 'I've been sorting out some study for you.' He held up a bunch of files and tossed them beside the books.

'Progress reports on my dig. Government propaganda on the advantages of nuclear power. The reasoned arguments we shall be presenting at the appeal. I think you'll find it all very useful.'

Raven still looked puzzled as the old man said patiently, 'It'll prepare the ground, as it were.'

The boy sensed that something was being planned for him, something demanded of him, of which he was only just becoming aware.

'You've only got a few weeks here, but you might as well involve yourself, don't you think? You'll have much more fun.'

Raven stared at the files and books with distaste. It would take him weeks to wade through that lot, and by that time it would be back behind wire netting, for him. Was that fun?

'First of all, I suggest you read up on the history of the area.' The Professor picked up a book and tossed it to Raven. 'I should start with this fellow, he'll give you the general picture…'

Raven pulled a face as he flicked through the pages. In some places the footnotes took up more of the page than the text! 'I thought this was supposed to be a holiday,' he complained.

The Professor's smile froze and suddenly he became very serious. 'Whatever gave you that idea?' he asked, as he wheeled away into the hall.

*

Raven pushed his cereal bowl to one side as Mrs Young put a heaped plate in front of him – fried eggs, bacon, sausages, tomatoes. That was one thing at least – the food was definitely superior to the Other Place. The Professor picked at a piece of dry toast.

'Listen, Prof. No offence, but this is your fight. What's it got to do with me, eh? I mean, I don't even agree with what you're trying to do.' He was surprised at the confidence in his voice.

Patiently the Professor explained. 'They're burying part of our national heritage under a nuclear waste reprocessing plant. And you call that progress?'

So the Professor had felt his needling? Raven grinned to himself. 'But it's got to go somewhere, hasn't it? Stands to reason.' He stabbed the sausage.

'What about the danger?' The Professor wiped his mouth with his napkin. 'Did you know that because of previous nuclear explosions, every single person on this planet – and that includes you – now has, in his body – your body – a minute quantity of plutonium? Man has already started to contaminate himself.'

Why did the old man always make him feel nervous? Now he was trying to tell him he was a walking bomb. Rubbish. 'That's why they want to stick it underground. So there'll be no more fall-out. It'll be safe down there.'

The Professor stared at him across the table. 'For hundreds of thousands of years? For the rest of time?'

The boy shrugged and buttered some toast. 'They wouldn't bother if they weren't sure, would they?'

The old head smiled at him. 'I wish I could share your optimism.' There he was again, treating him like a kid who had asked for too many toys.

Raven attacked. 'And think of the jobs it'll provide.

Think of the money it'll bring to the district. Think of the future.' Wasn't that the way Bill had put it to that newspaper girl?

The Professor looked grim. 'I am thinking of the future,' he said slowly.

'No, Prof. You're buried in the past, that's your trouble. Just like them caves of yours.'

There was a silence and Raven wondered if he had gone too far.

Mrs Young poured them all fresh coffee. 'I'm surprised at you, Raven. Surprised and disappointed...' murmured the Professor.

Raven waited. He had heard that sort of opening before. The remark was a gambit, not a chunk of opinion. The next move would be the surprise. Raven made the 'why' noises that were expected of him, and the Professor leapt in, predictably. 'That's the official line, the sort of cant I'd expect from a Ministry man.'

Raven was taken aback by this ploy.

'I thought you were something of a rebel. But it seems Borstal has knocked all the stuffing out of you.'

Raven suddenly realised that despite his tight defence, the old boy had scored – he could feel himself rising to the occasion, instead of playing it cool. 'You know what it said in my report? The one I nicked from the secretary's office? "Stubborn, independent, resentful of authority"... and you say my bottle's gone?'

The Professor waited for a moment before replying. 'If it hasn't, why are you talking like the establishment?'

It was a clever move that split the defence. Raven realised that backpedalling was about all that was left to him. He could wait out an attack of this sort. 'OK...' he stirred his coffee thoughtfully, 'I'll take a look at that stuff of yours. See what you're on about.'

The Professor did not relax. He leaned earnestly across the table. 'Read carefully. Try to keep an open mind.'

*

Raven read as carefully as he could. There was a great deal to read. Much of it repeated the arguments Bill had put forward and developed the arguments about which the Professor had droned on. What surprised the boy was that the material contained reasoned summaries of both sides of the question. That was fair of the old man. The local stuff was quite interesting and the cave reports were positively gripping in parts as they described the following-up of hunches – a bit like a good detective movie. Raven found that the hours sped by and the Professor was always available to explain the more difficult bits of the reports. In fact, Raven realised, he was a knowledgeable old bloke – particularly when he got carried away and started describing some aspect of his work down in the caves. Somehow it stopped sounding like a history lesson and started to grip the imagination.

The Professor ran a recording of a television pro-gramme in which he had recently appeared, discussing the whys and wherefores of the Governmental decision to build the reprocessing plant at his cave site. Raven sprawled across Bill Telford's desk, watching with interest. As the programme neared its end, it was curious to see the Portakabin shown on the screen as the camera panned around in a 360-degree shot of the great standing stones.

The voice of the presenter of the programme came over the pictures. 'Work continues on the site but the final decision as to whether or not this area should be developed for the benefit of both national and local interests remains in the balance, pending the Appeal. Not an easy decision but one which will have to be made soon.'

As the music swelled to a climax and the credits started to roll, the Professor leaned over and fast-forwarded the cassette, then removed it from the machine.

Raven was thoughtful, trying to balance in his mind all that he had learned during his crash-course. 'When did that go out?'

'Last week.' The Professor grinned rather sheepishly. 'I thought I came out of it quite well, didn't you?'

Raven slid off the desk, a worry lurking somewhere at the back of his head. He was aware that his position in the argument was no longer so positively pro-development. 'You're an amateur compared with that other lot. Them blokes from London in the sprauncy suits.'

The Professor caught something in the boy's tone. 'What do you mean?'

Raven stood, looking down at the model of the construction site and the standing stones which spread halfway across Telford's desk. 'It's no good going on about our heritage and stuff like that – they won't take a blind bit of notice.' He hesitated. What was he getting into?

The Professor urged, 'Go on.'

The boy shrugged. 'These geezers have got it together. They're hard – and you've got to be hard and all. Otherwise it's no contest.'

'So what do you advise?' The question was innocent but

the Professor had realised that he had achieved what he had set out to do in the education of the young fellow. Raven was interested… and he had kept an open mind.

Raven settled into his aggressive stance. 'Find out all you can about the opposition and put out some counter-propaganda. If the enemy is bent, try blackmail. If he's straight and especially if he's right, break a few legs.'

The impact of his words caught the Professor by surprise. It was the villainous practicality of them which startled a laugh out of him. The boy sounded like a pirate… a bandit chief.

Raven reacted to the laughter. 'Don't know what you're giggling about. The next battle's the Appeal, right? Lose that and you're in dead schtuck.'

The boy was right – that was what worried the Professor. The ruthless approach was much against his own nature but he was glad that the boy had demonstrated the necessity to carry the fight to the enemy. He was the right chap, after all.

Raven realised that he had been shooting his mouth off rather belligerently and grinned self-consciously. The Professor could not help grinning back. So much had been achieved in such a short time.

*

The old bike rattled and groaned its way through the town traffic. Raven caught sight of himself once or twice reflected in shop windows as he weaved through the cars and exhaust fumes. One thing about bicycles of doubtful vintage: one sat so high in the saddle that even bus drivers were almost eye to eye with you. Raven waited at a traffic light, watching the pedestrians stream by, and suddenly realised what an urban bloke he was at heart. The city, the town, was more his scene... people. He had enjoyed these past few days with the Youngs in a way that he could never have imagined prior to his arrival, but there was certainly something thrilling at being back in a town again. He leaned the bike against the wall beneath the huge plate-glass window that bore the legend *MIDSHIRES HERALD*.

Naomi Grant crossed the room to her desk. On the wall above her swivel chair was a complex mediaeval astrological chart, very decorative and very phoney. She cleared a space among the clutter and started to type but her eye was suddenly caught by a sight which bothered her for a moment. In the Editor's glassed-in booth Raven was being waved into a chair. They were talking animatedly but Naomi could not make out what was being said. She picked up her desk-phone and hit an intercom button to the receptionist. 'Julie... who's with the old man?'

The squawk confirmed her surprise. 'Yes. Did he say what he wanted?'

'What? Oh, nothing... yes, I know him...'

The Editor worked while Raven spoke. He was a hardboiled newspaperman and had sat through the enthusiasms of youth before.

'...And what about the Harland report?'

He looked wearily up at the boy. 'What about it?'

Raven began to hate him. 'It's an independent survey, innit?' The man's attitude made him lapse defensively into his own jargon. He had resolved to talk as 'posh' as possible but the geezer had got straight up his nose with his condescension.

'Independent?' The Editor threw his ballpoint on the desk and felt about him for his lost cigarettes. 'It was commissioned by Professor Young.' There was a sneer in his voice.

'It says the Government was wrong to choose that site.'

'It says the Government was wrong to choose any site.' The Editor stared at the boy, wondering just how much of the issue he really understood. 'It's against the whole principle of nuclear power.'

Raven held the glance. 'They haven't got the moral right, have they – the Government – they haven't got the moral right to...' He searched through his memory for the exact phrase from the Report. '...to endanger the lives of future generations?'

The Editor groped among the papers for his pen. 'I don't need you to quote the Report to me, Mr Raven.' He pulled a fresh batch of copy towards him. 'As it happens, I was at school with Harland, so I know just how full of his own self-importance he is.' He savagely struck out a whole paragraph of someone's purple prose.

Raven laughed. 'Well, that's tasty, innit? You won't listen to him because he nicked your ruler back in the Dark Ages?'

The Editor pushed away his work and settled back in his chair. 'Know anything about newspapers, do you, Mr Raven?'

'Not a lot.'

'Then you can't have any idea how difficult it is, holding down a job like this. The different interests that have to be taken into account...'

The smoke cloud again. The boy peered through it.

'What interests?'

The butt was stubbed out nervously in an ashtray that certainly needed emptying.

'An Editor has to be a juggler. He has to satisfy his proprietor, his advertisers and his readership.'

A compromiser, thought Raven. The world is full of them. They justify their existence constantly, claiming that compromise is what makes the world go round. Settling for less than their ideal, less than the best possible. They call it adult thinking. 'You mean you have to write what you're told to write? Not what you believe to be true?'

The chair rocked forward and the Editor's gaze wavered. 'Sometimes. Something like that… but I happen to believe that nuclear power is here to stay – that this reprocessing plant is going to be built somewhere, so it might as well be built here, on our patch. The benefits to the community will be enormous.'

There it was, the justification – the benefits, the money. 'And what about the damage? What about the demolition job they're doing on all that farmland? The waste of all them caves? They're going to shove stuff down there that'll still be dangerous in a quarter of a million years' time.'

The Editor smiled at the boy's passion. 'You have been doing your homework.'

'And they're burying our history and all. We shouldn't let them get away with it.'

Raven stopped to draw breath. There was a pause while the Editor stood up, inviting the boy to bring the interview to an end. 'Look, Mr Raven, I admire you for coming to see me – it shows that there are some youngsters who think about other things than taking football grounds apart – but even if I changed my policy, it wouldn't make the slightest bit of difference. The other side's got all the heavy artillery.'

Raven settled more comfortably in his chair, waiting for the frown of annoyance. 'So you're not going to try?'

'No.'

'Because your readers wouldn't like it? And they'd stop buying your paper?'

The Editor sat again, heavily. 'There's no point in discussing this further. The cause is already lost.'

The boy turned grim. 'Not yet, it ain't.' He went to the door. 'Harland may have been pretty unpleasant, but I bet you were a right crawler…' He had to grin as he watched the Editor's face start to purple.

The copyboy dropped mail into Naomi's in-tray as Raven left the Editor's booth. Naomi called him by name. 'You look as though you want to thump someone. What are you doing here?'

She looked surprised and worried for him. Raven realised that the Editor was watching them both from his office-booth, so he put on a smooth swagger which he did not really feel and nodded to the chart on the wall above Naomi's head. 'Astrology. You into all that?' He hoped the Editor would be wondering what on earth he was chatting to the girl reporter about. Worrying about it too, if possible.

Naomi tossed him a bunch of clippings. 'Madame Futura, that's me. I write the weekly horoscopes.'

Raven grinned. 'You knew I was coming, then?'

Naomi's eyes narrowed. What on earth was the lad doing here? 'I seem to remember you telling me that you weren't interested in the time-bomb they were planting under our feet.'

Raven shrugged. 'I wasn't clued up on the situation then, was I?'

'And now you are?'

Depression struck as he saw the Editor lose interest and return to his work. 'Yeah… maybe… well, it was worth a try, anyway.'

The girl was certainly as attractive as the first time they had met. She seemed genuinely interested, too. Maybe he should make more of an effort to be nice to her, try to impress a bit… Raven sat on the edge of her desk. 'You're two goals down away from home – so what do you do?'

She looked thoughtful, lost. 'I've no idea.'

'You pressurise your opponents, shove ten men into their penalty area. First thing we learned at Ferndown.'

Naomi noted the name on her pad. 'Best form of defence is attack?'

'Exactly. Stick one on them before they can put the boot in.'

The girl tossed her pencil aside. 'Problem here is we are two goals down, the boot is in, and the opposition won't be standing exactly still in their own penalty area.'

There was something odd about this girl. 'So what do you reckon?' he said. She sparkled when she started thinking – she looked good, scratching her head like that.

She smiled up at him, suddenly aware of his interest. Softly, she said, 'I don't know what's brought you around to this way of thinking but I'm glad. We'll have to work out a game plan of our own, keep on the attack. We've got to do what we can.'

Raven was dazzled by her breathless smile. He swallowed hard. 'We?' he bleated.

Naomi nodded firmly and punched him on the shoulder. 'We,' she said and grinned.

Chapter Four

MRS YOUNG STIRRED THE SOUP for lunch. She was hot and flustered and confused. The boy had been gone since early morning, leaving no word. She had seen him riding off down the drive on her old bicycle and had called to him but he had either not heard her from the upstairs window, or more likely had ignored her fussing.

The Professor wheeled himself into the kitchen to be met by the full blast of her frustrated worry. 'I don't understand you, James. You shouldn't have let him go off alone. He doesn't know his way about.'

The old man placed himself at the head of the table and waited patiently for food. He was peckish and in good humour. 'He's not a child. He's a young adult, my dear. We musn't keep him on too tight a rein.'

There he was again, being unreasonably calm. He was an infuriating husband. 'But we're responsible for his welfare.' She burned her hand on the lid of the pot and set it down heavily on the kitchen table.

The Professor breathed in the aroma and sliced himself a doorstep from the hot brown loaf beside him. 'I thought your intention was to help him readjust… to take his place in society?'

He was laughing at her. Of course, he was right – she was worrying unnecessarily. 'Did he say where he was going?' she asked.

The Professor shook his head.

A new thought struck her. Perhaps it was the fear that had been lurking in her heart all the time. 'What if he doesn't come back…?' That would be terrible, if the boy absconded. There would be so much trouble: for him, mainly, but she would also feel that she had failed hopelessly.

'He'll be back.' The Professor cooled the soup on his spoon, savouring the steam. 'He'll be back.' He sounded confident, almost as if he knew where the boy was, almost as if he was just teasing her. 'After all, how could he resist your cooking, my dear?'

Mrs Young smiled foolishly at her husband. There was no answer in his eyes and there was just a thought in her head that he had planned to say something more but had changed his mind. She stared across the table at him; he was, just for a moment, serious and somehow watchful. His eyes were like a bird's, like a hawk's…

*

The plastic cup was hot, the coffee as filthy as ever. Naomi nibbled on a bar of chocolate, glad that it took the taste away. Her editor glanced at her over the rim of his plastic cup. 'He's an interesting case. What do you make of him?'

Raven had not been out of their minds since he had left. A boy of his age attempting to get something done in an issue of this magnitude did not often come their way. And he had rather shaken the Editor by his grasp of the salient points at debate and with the fervour with which he had supported his cause. It was, they had to agree, a healthy sign that youth had something to contribute to the fight that was coming.

'He makes me fat.' Naomi finished the chocolate and sucked none too daintily at her fingers. 'It's that energy of his… it makes me nervous. When I get nervous, I eat.'

They both laughed. Naomi went on, 'But I want to follow up on his background. He mentioned Ferndown – that's a Borstal.' She grinned at the Editor in a way that began to get him nervous – she was after something, he thought. Her approach was altogether too casual: as devious as he had once been with his editor, at her age.

'You play golf with the Chief Inspector, don't you?'

She will undoubtedly make a first-class journalist one day, thought the Editor: a good mind allied to a good nose for a story and a winning way in eliciting information was a great basis from which to launch a career in the press.

'Do you lose regularly?' She was going for the Borstal angle, then.

'Reasonably often.'

'Shrewd. So he'll do us a check?' She tossed the cup into the waste-paper basket. At the door, she turned and gave a beaming, confident smile. 'I'll give him your love.'

He'll do her a check, thought the Editor. No one could resist that smile, least of all Chief Inspector Allen. He grinned at her as she grabbed her bag and almost ran from the main office. She'll do, he thought.

*

Raven stormed through the hallway into the Professor's study. It was empty. He hurriedly gathered together the books and files that the Professor had let him read – he had realised on the ride back from the newspaper offices that there was much more preparation to do if he was to convince anybody of the worth of his new-found cause. Naomi's help would, of course, be invaluable but one dolly bird was not much of an army.

As he fled up the stairs, two at a time, he heard the kitchen door open. Mrs Young came into the hallway and called, 'Oh, there you are, Raven. I've something to show you.' She sounded relieved, in some way. However, he did not need diversions just now and kept going, pretending not to hear. As his bedroom door closed behind him, he could still hear his name being called.

He tossed the reading matter on the bed and ripped off his bomber jacket. This was going to take planning, thinking through logically. He sat on the edge of the bed, head in hands.

There was a knock on the door and the handle turned, without waiting for his invitation. Mrs Young stood in the doorway holding yet another of those glass cases. What had she come up with this time?

'I thought you might like to have this.'

She placed the cased bird alongside the merlin's glass dome, and Raven's irritation disappeared as he saw what it was that she had brought… 'Terrific!'

It was a stuffed raven.

'You did tell me he was a member of the family. Kept you from harm as a baby – the only creature who seemed to care what happened to you.' She sounded tentative, wondering how he would react.

Raven reached for his photograph of the raven and compared it with the mounted specimen. They were practically identical.

Mrs Young could feel the boy's pleasure, his genuine joy in response to her gift. 'There he is, then. Still standing guard. It's not too morbid, I hope...' The thought had been worrying her.

Raven grabbed her and planted a kiss on her cheek. 'Morbid? You're a cracker, missus. It's what I've always wanted – a stuffed Dad!'

From its dome, the raven looked on enigmatically...

*

Naomi spoke into her deskphone. 'Yes, OK, Julie... send it through.' She rose and crossed the office towards the Editor's booth as the copyboy came towards her. As she passed him, she snatched the proferred manilla envelope, smiling him her thanks. She ripped open the report and quickly scanned the three pages as she made her way into the sanctum.

She whistled softly to herself and tossed the pages onto the desk in front of her boss. He looked at her but she was poker-faced, lost in thought. He picked up the police report and read it quickly, frowning.

'What's he trying to prove? This reads like the Nuremberg War Crimes.' He was genuinely astonished. Raven's police record was extraordinary even for a tearaway of his age.

Naomi left it for a moment, then said quietly, 'Angle. He's an orphan... how about *Rebel Finds Cause*?'

The Editor shook his head, re-reading salient moments from the report. 'Corny.'

Naomi reacted hotly, 'Not as hack as your effort last week. *Farmer Marries Childhood Sweetheart* – I mean, I ask you...'

Her boss threw the report on the desk. 'The kid'll soon get bored. When he finds out what he's up against, he'll be back playing football like the rest of them.'

Naomi knew he was wrong. There was something tougher, more original about this lad. 'Can I see what I can do with it?' she asked.

The Editor got up from the desk and put on his jacket. 'As long as it doesn't interfere with your other work.' He checked his watch and headed for the door and an appointment at the other side of the town. He would just make it, if he hurried.

'Weddings, funerals and horoscopes,' enquired Naomi drily. 'As if I'd let anything interfere with top-priority stuff like that.'

He ushered her out of the booth and across the main office. 'OK, try it. But I don't promise anything.'

He was gone but Naomi grinned and called after him, 'I don't care what they say. I think you're a very nice man.'

*

Raven sprawled across his bed, quickly revising the material that he had gathered from the Professor's study, trying to find a pattern of attack, a direction in which the

Government's aims for the reprocessing project were most suspect. As he switched his attention to another part of the filed report, his gaze caught that of the merlin in its glass case. It seemed to be watching him with beady approval. 'Dad' looked down at him too, enigmatic and thoughtful. The boy grinned to himself. He was getting too fanciful for his own good.

Mrs Young was busy in the kitchen, and the Professor was working at his study desk, apparently cataloguing material and writing up the day's report of the progress of his work at the cave site. The house was silent, its three occupants separately engrossed in their tasks.

The Professor's great, wise head lifted from his work as he became aware of Raven passing down the stairs and across the doorway, heading for the kitchen. Mrs Young looked up from her baking as Raven entered.

'Something smells good...' The boy sounded hungry and appreciative.

'Chicken casserole,' she said with a smile. 'I hope you like it.'

Raven moved to the Aga, nose sniffing the marvellous promise of the simmering pots. 'Love it. Eat anything, me. Fish, fur or feather. Ready soon, is it?' Suddenly he was starving.

There was the almost silent swish of tyres as the Professor wheeled himself into the room. He looked apologetic. 'Don't get too excited about supper – I have to get back to the site.'

Mrs Young looked flustered, and the annoyance showed in her voice. 'Why? What have you forgotten this time?'

'The slides.' Her husband looked almost sheepish and

stole a glance at Raven who was amused at the sight of the couple getting tetchy with each other over such a minor matter. 'I need them for this week's report – I must finish it tonight. I'm sorry.' The Professor's smile was genuine; he hated to put his wife out in any way.

She softened. 'Never mind... I'll get the car out.' She moved to rearrange the pots on the stove. Luckily the food would not spoil for some extra cooking.

Raven hesitated. He felt diffident about offering help; in fact, he felt that it was quite a new part of his nature showing – at the Home it was every man for himself. 'I'll go,' he heard himself say. 'Won't take me long on the bike. I can be back in no time.'

Mrs Young protested that it was too dark and that the site would be locked up but the Professor interrupted quickly. 'Good idea. You've got your pass and ID in case you meet the security chaps?' He tossed Raven a large bunch of keys. 'Main gate's the big one, alarm's the red one and the cabin's the one with the blue disc.' He grinned as a thought occurred to him. 'Although it may hurt your professional pride, I'd prefer you to use the keys, rather than practise your breaking and entering techniques!'

Raven grinned back. It seemed almost that the old man had set up this night return to the cabin. Raven wondered what the game was.

'You're looking for a box marked *CAVE SYMBOLS*, a photographic slide box – it's in the cabinet.'

There was a challenge in the Professor's gaze as Raven moved for the door. The boy could not yet see what the Professor was being so mysterious about. It was a complicated way of getting him out of the house – just

when he badly needed supper, too. He tore the heel off a
French loaf that lay on the table. 'This'll keep me going till I
get back – don't eat all that chicken.' And he went out into
the dark of the night.

*

He pushed the bike the last few yards, through the gate and
up to the Portakabin. It fell to the ground as he tried to lean
it against the cabin wall and he left it where it lay, the back
wheel spinning insanely. It was too dark to mess about with
a wreck that did not want to stand up. He fiddled with the
keys, trying to find the right one.

The door swung open and Raven reached inside for the
light. He stood blinking in the doorway for a moment.
There were papers lying on top of the filing cabinet but he
could see that there was no photographic slide container.
He started a general search around the desk area. Nothing.
Nothing on the drawing board. He tried the filing cabinet
but the drawers were locked and none of the keys on his
bunch fitted. The boy kicked the tin box viciously, it would
take him thirty seconds to break into it but there was no
point. The Professor would never have sent him this far
without keys and with the wrong instructions if the slides
were inside a locked filing cabinet... or would he? There
was something not altogether sane about this entire
venture.

The answer was easy. He picked up the telephone and
dialled the Youngs' number. When in doubt, ask. It was at
that moment that he caught sight of a corner of a likely-
looking box sticking out from under some papers lying on
the telescreen set-up. He put down the phone, opened the

box and checked one of the slides, but even near a light he found it impossible to see clearly what the slide depicted. The box was unmarked and he had no way of telling whether this batch of slides were the ones the Professor needed – if indeed the slides were the real reason that the Professor had sent him on this search at all. Still, whatever the old man's reasons, it would seem futile to return with a box of slides that had no relevance to the report.

Raven suddenly spotted the slide carrier on the tele-unit on which the Professor had shown him one or two slides yesterday. Was it yesterday? He was losing track of time in this confusing place. He dropped a few slides into the holder and fumbled among the switches. Some were marked and he worked logically through the necessary ones. He waited for a warm-up period but nothing happened: there was still a dead feeling about the electronics. Suddenly realisation dawned and, feeling rather idiotic, Raven reached for the mains switch. Moments later a monitor flickered into life and slowly, the picture resolved itself into a crudely carved Celtic cross.

Frowning, Raven switched slides and up came another – this time a piece of broken pottery held by a girlish hand. These were definitely the wrong slides. He switched quickly through the remainder, all similar finds. As he removed the offending articles and returned them to their box he realised that for some moments he had been aware of faint, far-away music.

The boy froze, listening, wondering, then he realised that the beautiful, seductive sounds were coming from the tele-speaker. He reached forward rather tentatively and turned up the sound control. The cabin filled with noise.

Mixed with the faint, haunting music was a babble of inarticulate sound – voices, the sound of fractured laughter, footsteps. Harness jingled at the stamp of horses' hooves. There was the sound of metal on metal, the fluttering of wings – and below, above and throughout it all, the strange, lilting, unmatchable tune – a melody that caught at his heart but which he could not follow in his mind although he ached to do so. Raven felt that what he heard was coming from another time, another dimension... of the Earth but not of now...

He carefully punched up the monitors, one by one. As each screen cleared, there was only blackness. The boy hit the lighting switches and the caves below flooded with light. As his eyes flicked from screen to screen searching for the source of the beautiful, mysterious sounds, a ghosting effect began to take shape on each monitor... nothing definite, shapes melting, shadows moving, somehow related to the shapes that he was hearing.

Raven tried to pin down the meaning of the phantoms on the screens. He was as though hypnotised, not sure if what he saw and heard had any real existence or whether it was just storm-dreams hunting across the confusion of his mind. The sound was growing, the pictures forming and swirling away in more recognisable patterns. Suddenly – was it in his head or on a screen? – Raven saw a face... the face of a young man, a young man that he knew well. The face was full of wisdom – it glowed with youth and yet the knowledge of age; it had an aspect that was... royal...

He fought against the turmoil that was in him, tore his eyes away from the monitor screens, clapped his hands over his ears and screamed to make the sounds go.

The music swelled in volume, the pictures faded away to be replaced with a symbol that he had never seen before. It gradually took shape and filled the screen before fading forward into his mind where it burnt an image of itself, indelible and ineradicable. The symbol was thus:

Raven stared at the dead screens, the empty caves, the echo of silence. He felt his fear recede, his strength return. And with it, the unbearable sense of loss – the loss of something greater than himself, something more desirable than his ambitions, something sweeter than anything he had ever dreamed.

And in his heart was the knowledge which he fought, which he could not encompass, which his mind would not let him admit to be possible or true. The face which he had seen, the calm, terrible face of the young king, was his own…

*

Raven stumbled out of the Portakabin, drawn by an impulse that was beyond reason. He raced through the darkness to the entrance of the cave shaft.

Habit, some obedience built-in in response to instruction, made him struggle into a suit and helmet before he entered the lift and crashed the gates behind him.

When they opened again at the bottom of the shaft, the echoes cut through the silence of the deserted caves. Then the silence swallowed the harsh sounds and reimposed its will. The bright lights hurt the boy's eyes and somehow emphasised the emptiness of the caverns.

He moved quickly, silently through into another part of the system… nothing. His mouth was dry with the fear of the unknown. Why had he come here? Nothing had any real meaning in his mind any more. He cleared his throat and called, 'Where are you…?'

As the *are you… are you… are you…* faded its echoes around the workings, he realised that he had never meant to say such a thing. He did not know why he had asked the question – he had not known what he was going to say when he had opened his mouth, but he just knew that he needed to break the silence, to reassert the reality of his existence.

The boy entered a small slip, a narrow cleft leading into another chamber. He stumbled and suddenly gasped: the slip seemed longer than he remembered, the chamber further than he recalled. He knew that curiously he was suddenly cold, although he could feel sweat run from beneath the peak of his helmet into his eyes. He sucked in air, desperately.

Then he remembered… he looked down at his chest, to the gas telltale that was sewn into the suit. He tried desperately to focus his melting mind on the meaning of the growing red mark that spread across the…

Concentrate. Move. Gas-pocket… Move… One leg. Fall. He had fallen badly against the side wall and was aware of the sharp uneven surface cold upon his cheek. Crawl. That was it… perhaps low down he was safer. Perhaps… faster. No more… he knew he could go no further…

Pride forced him to his feet. He found that he was clear of the slip, into the silence of the small chamber. All that remained in his head was the question he had not meant to ask, the question whose answer he dreaded… 'Who are you?'

The echoes crashed back at him and he knew he had used the last of his reserves. The blackness came, welcome and sweet and the boy slid away to the brink of eternity.

*

In the caves the lights snapped off. Total darkness, the darkness of the old Earth returned. The echoes of the boy's voice drifted about the furthest caverns, idly, it seemed – not wanting to die.

In the darkness, far away, the symbol formed:

The voices and the music approached from somewhere in time, coming, lilting from the past… this time, here and now, around each corner, close at hand…

Raven's body, starved of air, slumped along the chamber wall, fell backwards into a niche and was held upright, almost as if he were seated, casually, on a throne.

His eyes stared unseeing as the music increased in

beauty, in triumph – as the phantasms took shape and the symbol approached, part of the very air, dominating the life-force that was born within the chamber.

Raven felt within him the need to live: the urgent will returned to his mind, casting out the peace of oblivion. He sat still, struggling to breathe, to see, to think...

The ghosting figures became his reality. He peopled them with the attributes of those he knew. He made them his friends, hallucinatory versions of Naomi, Bill...

The Professor approached, holding out his hands to him, smiling... that was impossible, even his mind knew that the Professor was crippled, could not walk. He cast the phantasm out of his world. It changed its being to someone he had never seen... a young man, muscular, confident but somehow holy. Others crowded in and all the time the sounds were eating at his heart. Blackness began to return to his mind and the only knowledge lay in the gathering symbol.

The music sharpened and the fluttering of black wings breathed air into his retching lungs. Time had gone... he was following it fast...

Towards him came the final moment of his young life – the figure he had seen before, the one terrifying and fearsome ordeal of his first vision... himself... and yet not himself... not yet himself... The young king came to him and stretched out his arm. The silence in Raven's head refused to listen to the crescendo of music that crashed around the caverns. The beautiful young king touched the boy's forehead with his outstretched thumb and the growing symbol swallowed them all into its blackness...

*

Raven staggered out of the lift as the gates crashed back, and stumbled, tired as death, retching for air, along the tunnel towards the fresh, first night of his life…

He reeled across the construction site, not caring, tearing his lungs with the sweet icy draughts of necessity. He staggered on, wanting to laugh his heart awake again, wanting to scream his mind into obedience. His new knowledge must be filed, used, tasted before it faded… and it was going fast, too fast.

He fell and lay still, luxuriating in the comfort of grass and a chill wind that sliced across his body.

It seemed like hours later, though it may only have been moments, that he stirred and raised his head, needing to know where he was. Staring down at him was the great crude shape of a bird. He rose and staggered, looking around him wildly. He was surrounded by gigantic shapes… a woman… a lion… a bull's head. He began to realise where he was and the panic in him passed.

He was at the centre of the great stone circle. The huge shapes loomed above him. He cast about in the darkness for a direction, a way back to the world. He found the lights of the Portakabin streaming across the site behind him. He gasped with relief, tired now as he had never been before… He started towards the cabin but stopped suddenly as his heart lurched in his body. Between him and the light, black against the brightness, stood the Professor's wheelchair. Empty…

Chapter Five

INSIDE THE PORTAKABIN, THE PROFESSOR sat before the bank of television screens, punching up one subterranean cave after another. Mrs Young stood behind him, peering anxiously over his shoulder.

'Cave nine, empty… cave ten, empty… eleven, empty…' The old man leaned back in his chair, looked up at his wife and shrugged helplessly.

She shook his arm violently. 'He's down there somewhere… he must be. The lift's at the bottom of the shaft.'

The Professor warmed her with a smile. It was an ease he did not wholly feel. 'Don't worry, my dear. He's not in any danger.'

'Suppose he's buried under a fall of rock or something?' She searched in her handbag for a tissue. She hoped she was not going to cry but she was genuinely worried now. The evening had taken a strange bothersome turn since James had sent the boy on his night errand.

'If there'd been a rockfall, we'd have seen it on a monitor. No, he's perfectly safe.' Where did the justification for his words come from, he wondered? Deep inside himself, he knew he was right even though all the portents told him to worry.

Suddenly the door burst open and Raven appeared.

He leaned against the wall and stared wild-eyed at the Professor. Mrs Young gasped at the boy's condition. She went to him quickly and led him to a seat. The power went from his legs but not from his growing anger. Although he didn't know how, somehow he felt that it had all been the fault of the old man. 'What's your game, Prof?' he challenged.

'My poor boy – are you all right?' Mrs Young fussed about him, removing the helmet. His hair was stuck to his head with sweat. 'You look dreadful…'

The Professor cut across her: 'Game?' He sounded relieved but petulant. Had the boy experienced nothing? Where had he been?

There was a silence as Raven tried to make sense of the situation. 'The chair. Why aren't you in your wheelchair?'

There was a slight laugh from Mrs Young as she soaked a tissue at the small plastic sink in the corner of the cabin. The Professor glanced at her and explained, 'The ramp's been moved, and my wife had to lift me inside.' He seemed puzzled by the nature of the question. Surely there were more important things to discuss.

'So what was it doing out there in the middle of the Stone Circle?' The boy dropped the question in the air between them like something too fragile to handle. It had seemed so mysterious when he first stumbled on the chair, somehow, so significant of something. Now, he could see that the chair might well have rolled away from the cabin if the brake had not been properly applied, which was exactly what the old man confirmed.

Raven slumped in the chair, deflated, and Mrs Young bent over him solicitously, peering into his face.

'What's that on your face…?'

Raven looked at her, trying to find a witty reply but the strange look that she had as she studied his forehead stopped him. 'Is it a graze?' She rubbed at his forehead with the wet tissue and smiled, 'No…'

Raven felt something go from him. A faintness came over him and the lights in the cabin seemed to dim. He fought for consciousness and through the blur of swimming reality he saw… he thought he saw… the young king approach and reach out his thumb towards his forehead. This time he could see plainly that imprinted on the thumb of the young king was the symbol that haunted the caves.

The image faded and reality returned.

The Professor leaned forward excitedly. 'Do you remember?' he demanded, 'do you remember what happened? How you got that mark on your forehead?'

The quiet insistence irked Raven. How was he to explain his dream sequence to the old man? Better to keep all that to himself. It was part of his private world. But what did the Professor know about it? Raven saw in his glance that he knew something.

'I remember nothing,' he lied. He took the Professor's glance and held it, fearlessly. He had been taught to lie like this at the Home. Lie truthfully, be bold – he had been taught by experts.

The Professor recognised the lie and broke the tension between them. 'What made you go down to the caves?' he asked more gently.

Raven was glad to be let off the hook. 'I thought I heard… noises.'

Mrs Young, flustered, shrugged off her topcoat. 'Noises?'

Raven turned to her. 'Through the speaker. Then, when I switched on the monitor…' The effort of trying to rise and go to the Professor's side made his head swim again and in that moment he saw again in his mind the vague figures of his vision. It was a sort of warning moment, he felt.

The boy shrugged. 'Forget it. It must have been ghosting… signals from another frequency.'

The Professor was about to protest, for he had noticed Raven's change of direction but the door opened and Bill Telford entered, jacket and trousers over his pyjamas. His temper seemed none too good.

'Emergency, eh? This'd better be good, Professor.' He glared at Raven, too. 'What's it all about?'

The Professor leaped in with his apology. 'I'm sorry, Mr Telford… I'm afraid it's a false alarm.' He tried to smile but he got little response from the irate construction boss.

'False alarm? You mean you ruined my beauty sleep for nothing?' Bill sounded disbelieving. Something had happened and he wanted to know what it was.

'We had a lost sheep. Luckily, he's turned up safe and sound.' The Professor sounded most anxious to placate and Bill wondered why. He turned to Raven.

'You? What have you been up to, then?'

The boy looked tired and felt worse. 'I went down to the caves. Suddenly I couldn't breathe. Must've blacked out for a bit.'

The Professor leaned forward, his eyes fixed on Raven's chest. 'Look at his telltale.'

Bill was beside the boy in a moment. He inspected the instrument carefully – the red sector was at an alarmingly high reading. He looked up at the Professor. 'Gas?' He sounded puzzled.

Raven decided he'd tell Bill all about it sometime. Apart from Naomi, whom he was sure would believe his story, Bill seemed to be the sort of practical man who might just understand such flights of fancy.

Bill shook him by the shoulders. This was important. 'Do you remember where it hit you?'

'I think so.'

'Show me.' He moved to the desk and grabbed a plan of the caves which he thrust at the boy. Raven studied it, trying to recall his movements. Of course, the slip – the narrow cleft between that cave and the smaller one. He pointed.

'There. Somewhere around there and in that traverse.'

Bill frowned at the plan. 'I'll have it checked out.' His anger was never far from the surface when he had been crossed – he admitted freely that he was that sort of man and now he turned on the Professor. 'You'd better keep your lot on a lead in future. If I catch any of them down there out of safe working hours, I'll put in an official complaint. You cause us enough trouble as it is.'

The Professor realised that he had failed to get through to the building man yet again. He winked ruefully at Raven, who decided that this was a good time to keep quiet.

*

Naomi passed the secretaries and crashed straight into the Editor's office. He was hunched over some copy but she did not let that cool her good humour. She perched on the corner of the desk, provocatively. 'Morning, boss…'

The Editor did not look up as he made a small adjustment to the words in front of him. 'Go away and play with your horoscopes. I'm busy. And don't call me boss.'

She grinned. 'Don't you want to hear about my scoop?'

He looked up sourly for a moment, then returned to his work. 'Scoop?' he muttered, 'My dear girl, reporters don't talk like that any more. You'll be telling me to hold the front page next.'

Naomi waited and the silence worried the man. He looked up and sighed, knowing he would get no peace until he had heard her out. He laid down the copy and straightened up in his chair. 'All right, what's this all about…?'

'Raven.'

Naomi watched the thoughts chase themselves across his face. It was as though she had tapped him sharply on the funnybone. He did not seem to know whether to laugh or cry first.

'Got something to show me? Something concrete?' He sounded resigned.

'Not yet. But he gets more and more interesting.' She shifted nearer to him on the desk and he grabbed at the ashtray that almost fell in his lap.

'I've talked to the Governor of Ferndown… Raven's out

on licence from Borstal.'

The Editor did not react in any way. She realised that he was not a bit surprised.

'No one seems to know who his parents were,' she ploughed on. 'He was found in a field with this bird beside him, which is how he got his name.'

The Editor's eyes narrowed. 'Sounds like a publicity gimmick.'

Naomi slid off the desk and tried to pace around the room but it was so small she could get nowhere in any direction. 'He needs publicity like a drowning man needs water. You've seen his record – he's been in trouble with the law ever since he could walk.' She could see a flicker of interest beginning in old Stoneface and went on quickly. 'So – now the eminent Professor Young takes him under his illustrious archaeological wing and suddenly he's a crusader. This story's got everything – the generation gap, the clash of cultures, bad boy makes good. It's got human interest written all over it.'

Naomi waited while the Editor chewed the end of his ballpoint. He shook his head but this time he was obviously not so sure. She knew she had got through to him.

'Bad boy makes good? As far as I can see he hasn't made anything but a nuisance of himself.' He was dithering, she felt sure.

'That's how you get things done, making a nuisance of yourself – a thorough nuisance. Sometimes you even get things not done.' She grinned and headed for the door, 'Watch this space...'

Her boss called, 'Where are you going?'

'To do some in-depth interviewing. Get the full

background to the heart-rending saga...' She slipped through the door and away.

He followed her and called across the noise of the typewriters in the office outside. 'If it goes against editorial policy, I won't print it.' But he had to admit, he was interested. It was possible, and a good one, too.

Naomi's head poked back into the main office from the corridor. 'Then I'll send it to one of the nationals!' and she was gone before he could respond. Damn the girl, she always wanted the last word, he thought – and she usually got it.

*

Raven sat slumped in the chair, chewing the end of his dressing-gown cord. He could hear the low voices from the hall, where the Professor and Mrs Young were seeing the doctor to his car. The front door closed as the Professor wheeled himself back into the study.

The old man regarded him oddly. 'The doctor says there's no internal damage – you had a lucky escape.'

Raven wondered what the Professor was really thinking of his adventure. The wheelchair spun to its place by the desk and the old man threw his next question back at the boy, behind him. 'Why are you looking at me like that?'

There was a long moment of silence while Raven fought to get his emotions in order. This had to be a 'serious' discussion, no point in plunging headlong into accusation and counter-ploy. It was time he let the Professor know what he thought and come to some understanding of the old man's role in his developing young existence... 'You knew I was going to go down into the caves, didn't you?' he began slowly. His voice was mild, matter of fact. 'You wanted me to go down there?'

The Professor turned to see his face, surprised by both the questions and the tone. He frowned, not quite sure of his stand in all this yet. 'Did I...?'

The boy nodded solemnly. 'And you know what I saw... and all...'

The Professor smiled a secret sort of smile. 'Perhaps.' He looked at the boy carefully, then as though he had made up his mind to tell something of importance, he went on quickly, 'I too was once trapped by what we thought was a gas pocket... down in those caves. Unfortunately, my experience led to an accident, when I panicked. That's why I'm confined to this chair...' His voice tailed away and his eyes became private for a while.

'So you saw what I saw!' Raven burst out excitedly.

There was a silence. Then the Professor sighed gently and said, 'No.'

The boy was lost now: the conversation was not going as planned and he had missed his way in amongst its implications. 'I don't get it.' He felt more helpless than ever.

The Professor turned to his work. 'It's not necessary for you to "get it", Raven. As long as you appreciate the importance of your task – that's all that matters.'

'What task?' The old man was wandering, thought Raven.

'To run. To go where I cannot go. To be at the right place at the right time. That's all... for the present.' He sounded certain, as though it were an order he was merely passing on from a higher authority.

This was getting maudlin. 'Sorry, Professor – you've lost

me.' If he was not going to be more specific…

'No matter. The time for understanding has not yet come. Perhaps after you've talked to your lady visitor…'

Now what was he going on about?

'Someone of whom you've become rather fond, I think. She's on her way to see you.' The old head was listening to the sound of an approaching car, carefully negotiating the lane.

It was certainly not Miss Pettigrew, thought Raven. That could only leave Naomi, but the Professor had never met her, had he?

'A word of advice, my boy. Don't become too fond of her. She's not for you.'

The doorbell rang and saved Raven's angry blushes. The old man's words had exposed to the boy feelings which he had not yet fully sorted out in his own mind and he reacted badly to this invasion of his privacy, particularly as the Professor could have no knowledge of what had passed between Naomi and himself, nor of the friendship that had grown between them. The boy decided that the old man was just taking a stab in the dark, trying to draw him out for some reason, and did not really know anything of his feelings for the girl. He decided to let him know nothing. Nothing at all.

Voices came from the hall as Mrs Young opened the front door. The sounds were muted but the Professor was right. That was Naomi's voice answering the old lady's questions. Neither the boy nor the Professor could hear the actual words used but the tones were unmistakeable.

'Come in, my dear,' the Professor sang out loudly. 'I can always make time for the Press.'

They waited and heard the front door close and the footsteps approach. Mrs Young opened the study door and ushered Naomi into the gloomy room. She stood in the doorway, trying to accustom her eyes to the light and Raven was once more struck by her presence. She was a knockout!

She grinned at him, then at the Professor. 'Thank you,' she said. Mrs Young closed the door and pottered off towards the kitchen. Naomi suddenly realised that Raven was in bedclothes and had not his usual snap and prance about him. She inspected him more closely... 'Hi,' she said, 'You look terrible.'

'He had a little accident last night, down in the caves.' The Professor showed her to a chair and she sat, gratefully.

'He looks as if he'll live...' she grinned.

Raven felt he was losing out on this meeting and there was something bothering him greatly. 'Tell me something, Tasty,' he tried. 'Have you ever met the Prof before?'

'I know of him by reputation and I've always wanted to do an interview with him but no... this is our first meeting, I think.' She wondered why Raven was looking not at her but at the Professor.

The old man smiled at Raven's obvious ploy and said quietly, 'I didn't tell you, Raven, but it was some time ago. Miss Grant is now too young to remember...'

*

Bill Telford came out of the narrow slip into the small chamber as the company geologist, Stone, was packing away the equipment.

'Nothing to worry about.' He sounded relieved. 'I've been pretty thorough, Bill. There might be an isolated pocket occasionally but the telltales should give the men plenty of warning.'

Bill kicked at a rock and it ricocheted off the cave wall. 'So there's only the natural element here?'

'Absolutely. Oxygen and nitrogen. Breathe it…' The stolid scientist grinned.

Bill kept going. 'Nothing toxic, nothing combustible? No danger?'

'Combustible?' Stone wondered at the naivety of the question. Bill knew that they would not be working here if any combustible gases had been suspected in the original survey, so what was he after? He shook his head, realising that he was being pinned down to a final decision. 'You'd need a pretty rare set of circumstances, believe me.'

'So I can tell the lads there's no danger?'

'You can tell them there's more danger crossing the road.'

Both men laughed, glad that the situation was resolved. They started to hump the test gear towards the lift shaft.

Stone asked, 'This lad – the one who says he blacked out. One of the Professor's lot, is he?'

Bill shook his head. 'Not officially. He's just… staying with him.'

'How old, would you say?'

'Fifteen, sixteen.'

The geologist nodded, 'That explains it. Highly developed imagination. Just the age.' They both jiggled the equipment into the lift. Bill climbed over the cases and closed the gates. 'You think he made the whole thing up?' He sounded doubtful, knowing Raven as he did.

Stone leaned across to punch the button and the lift

jerked into its rise. 'Methylhydroxylene is non-toxic, Bill. And in such small quantities there's no way it could have knocked him unconscious.'

*

Mrs Young had been and gone with coffee and the pleasantries had finished. Naomi had put on her working face and some of her questions had shaken Raven out of his attitude towards her of careless banter. She could be tough, he realised. Her notebook was rapidly filling with notes and quotes.

'So it was through the Professor that you first took an interest in ecology?'

Raven could not resist one last exasperation. 'The what?' he asked, innocently.

'The protection of the environment,' translated the young journalist. Then she looked up from her notes and saw that her leg was being pulled. She turned to the Professor, patiently. 'Was it difficult to convert him, Professor?'

'Convert?' The old man smiled at the boy fondly. 'What an odd word to choose. I merely helped him to open his mind. Convinced him that one cannot reject the past without endangering the future. That both are inextricably bound up with the present.'

Raven nodded. It had been something like that.

Naomi turned back to him. 'Can you give me a useable quote, Raven? About what this fight means to you?'

He hated being put on the spot like this. He shrugged: 'I just know it's important, that's all.' Even he was aware how feeble a quote that would make.

Naomi kept going. 'But why save the caves? What do you find important in that?'

He looked around him at the fragments of pottery and lumps of jumble-sale rubbish that the Professor treasured and that had probably been thrown away as useless five hundred years ago, and could think of no sensible answer to the girl's question. 'The carvings... they mean something,' he blurted out.

'Any idea what?' If only she would not write down everything. It was unnerving.

The Professor interrupted. 'You've seen the carvings, Miss Grant? Have you any theories?'

She shook her lovely head. 'I'm not an archaeologist, Professor.'

Raven watched the old man... he had caught a change of pace... a tone.

The Professor wheeled himself across the room towards a projector. 'What about your female intuition?' He nodded Raven towards the window, to shut out what little sunlight entered. Raven eased himself out of the armchair. 'Let's have a look at them again and see if anything occurs to you. I'd be glad of your help.' He smiled delightfully at the girl and she responded with interest.

Raven closed the interior shutters, plunging the room into darkness. As he did, the Professor started the machine and flashed up on the wall the first of the series of slides.

The old man, his face illuminated by spill from the projector, watched Naomi scribbling notes as the symbols appeared one by one. When he had gone through the entire set, he called, 'That's the lot... light, Raven,' and the boy revealed the sun once more.

Naomi was troubled. She read from her book: 'Unicorn... phoenix?... ram... bull... man... ship... lion... girl or woman... another bird, dove?... scorpion... and a serpent.'

The Professor waited a little before he asked, 'Any ideas?'

Naomi struggled with something that seemed to stir somewhere at the back of her understanding. 'Afraid not.'

'You don't recognise any of these symbols?' the old man urged. Raven wondered why he was so insistent on Naomi's help. It was almost as though he thought she really did have the answer to the riddle.

Naomi hesitated. She looked at the Professor doubtfully, then at Raven. 'The ram, the bull, the lion, they are all...' she trailed away, lost in thought.

'Go on.' The Professor sounded urgent.

'They are all signs of the Zodiac. Aries, Taurus, Leo...'

'Good.' The Professor beamed at Raven. 'What about the others?'

Naomi thought it through carefully. 'I suppose the girl could be Virgo, the dove could be Libra, the scorpion speaks for itself – but the others make no sense at all.' She bit her lip.

'Not now, perhaps – but they meant something to the carvers,' prompted the Professor.

Raven chipped in – he did not really know why he said it. 'Was the symbols always the same? Or was they different in them days? For the Zodiac, I mean...'

Naomi looked up at him, startled. 'Some of them were, yes. That's it! Aquarius used to be represented by a phoenix, Cancer was a ship, Gemini a giant...' She was really excited now… 'It is. It's a Zodiac…'

'Interesting.' The Professor sounded elated, too, but thoughtful. 'Some people have a theory that Arthur's Round Table was in reality a Zodiac…'

Raven and Naomi glanced at each other expectantly. Naomi tried to sort out her notes but ended up shaking her head over her book. 'There's just one thing wrong. There should be twelve symbols but there are only eleven.'

'Their positions are marked on the plan.' The Professor wheeled himself back to his desk and unfolded a large map of the cave system. Naomi and Raven peered over his shoulder. The symbols were marked in red and were easy to pick out.

Raven asked, 'Which one's missing?'

The girl flicked through the notes. 'Sagittarius. There's no Sagittarius…'

The boy shrugged, 'Perhaps they didn't have it in those days.'

Naomi protested, 'They did, though. It was represented by a centaur – half man, half horse.'

They studied the plan carefully. The boy muttered to himself, 'All right then, why did they leave out poor old Sagittarius?' Naomi shook her head, at a loss, and stood back squinting at the plan through half-shut eyes.

Raven suddenly went cold. Without taking his eyes from the chart he reached a hand behind him and said quietly, urgently, 'Give us a pencil, Prof.' He was worried in case he lost sight of something that appeared to be so obvious now.

The Professor wordlessly handed the boy a blue marker pen. Raven started to outline the entire cave system with a bold hand.

'What are you doing?' All Naomi could see was the boy destroying a valuable chart with his scrawling pen.

Raven finished and stood back. He grabbed Naomi's arm and moved her further away from the desk. 'Now. See anything?'

Raven had effectively drawn the shape of some sort of animal.

'Looks like a horse.' Naomi felt excited but sounded uncertain.

Raven grinned at the Professor. 'No way is that going to win the Grand National.'

'A dog, then?' Naomi tried.

Raven stood even further back. 'A dog with a forked tail?'

That brought the Professor into the conversation. He had seemed to be away somewhere in a world of his own. Now, without giving the chart a glance, he said, 'Forked tail, eh? How about a dragon?'

That was it. Obvious. That's what it was. A primitive dragon outlined by the shape of the entire cave system.

The Professor wheeled himself across and looked down at the plan thoughtfully, 'Extraordinary. Arthur... King Arthur – he was known as the Dragon King.'

Naomi and Raven glanced at each other, puzzled at the Professor's tone and the enigmatic look on his face. He had led them in this way and they had arrived at a discovery. But at a discovery of what?

Chapter Six

RAVEN FINISHED TELLING NAOMI ABOUT his 'accident' as they climbed out of her car beside the Portakabin and walked through the rock circle towards the head of the lift shaft. Raven noticed that Mrs Young's Mini leaned drunkenly nearby, so presumably the Professor was hereabouts.

The boy looked up at the looming rocks but they had lost the shapes that he had experienced on his night visit to the site. Now they were merely strange.

Naomi looked back and called him and Raven hurried to catch her at the mouth of the tunnel. Bill Telford stepped out of the lift while they were struggling into spare protective equipment. As he saw them, he stared at them with barely veiled hostility.

'Got your passes, have you?'

He would not take their word but insisted on seeing them. He almost snarled as he warned them about their behaviour and told them to keep well clear of his workers.

'What's up with him, then?' Raven stared after his friend.

Naomi adjusted her helmet as they climbed into the lift. 'Must've given him a scare, you running into that gas pocket. He could have found himself out of a job.'

'You reckon that's all he cares about?' Raven sounded hurt. He could not understand Bill's sudden antipathy.

'It's a six-year project, Raven. And there's a lot of unemployment in the construction industry.' Naomi did not sound totally convinced, however. 'But it's more than that. He really believes that knocking down old monuments is progress, and that anyone who tries to stop him is some kind of maniac.'

She turned to see Raven grinning at her. 'Know something?' he said. 'You're even tastier when you get worked up!'

Not altogether displeased with the compliment, Naomi growled 'Come on,' and led the way out of the lift into the cave system.

There were a few construction workers about and they kept well clear of them, threading their way past in single file as quickly as possible and heading into the further cave. As they passed into the depths of the complex, Raven caught sight of several of the carved symbols. He twigged Naomi, 'How about those horoscope things of yours, then? Do you really believe in all that nonsense?'

She glanced shrewdly at him. Did she? It was a question she had asked herself many times without ever coming up with a totally convincing answer. He obviously did not. The phrase *a load of rubbish* was already waiting on his lips for her next question. She decided to bypass the argument. 'Tell you what – I'll work out your horoscope and you can see how accurate astrology can be. When's your birthday?'

Raven shrugged. 'Dunno, really. They reckoned it was probably sometime in early December. I've never bothered with birthdays and that...' He sounded wistful, even to himself.

Naomi had stopped and looked at him thoughtfully. 'Well, well... the missing link. You're the Sagittarian.'

Raven stared at her. So what? So he's the only one without a cave. Tough. I started life, he thought, with an earthmaze of my own. That's one up on a cave.

Naomi held his gaze. 'You know what Zodiac means... literally?'

Raven looked blank.

'Animals. The word comes from the Arabic.' Now why hadn't that occurred to her while she was with the Professor? Maybe he could have made something of that rather than going off into his Arthurian phase.

'Animals, eh?' Raven stared up at the lion symbol carved above the entrance to the next cave. Naomi could not tell what was going through the boy's mind.

She asked, 'Tell me a bit more about these hallucinations of yours. Whereabouts were you?'

Without moving, he indicated the lion-cave. 'In there,' he said quietly and led the way to the mouth of the slip looking through into the chamber. Above the entrance was carved the symbol of the dove.

Naomi nodded at it and said, 'The girl that you thought you saw... she was in that cave?'

She looked worried and moved through the slip into the

small cavern. Raven followed her tentatively and could not help glancing down at the telltale to see if the red was creeping across its face... but all was normal, all was well.

'It's a coincidence, you know,' said Naomi. 'The dove... it's the symbol for Libra.' She turned to Raven and said simply, knowing that he would understand the full significance of her statement, 'I'm a Libran.'

He shrugged it off with the brashness of his youth. 'Must've been dreaming of you, then.'

Naomi tried to go along, to play the game, but she did not feel the truth was in it. 'You must be careful who you let into your dreams...'

That was a new and amusing thought to Raven. He stopped and looked at her more carefully. 'Why? What do you mean by that?'

The girl hesitated, looked away up the slip and murmured, 'They could be a disappointment.' She felt shy suddenly, out of her depth.

Raven pressed, 'You mean, they might not want to be dreamed of?'

She turned back to face him, troubled now. 'I mean, it might be an honour that they could not live up to.'

They stared at each other in unspoken intimacy. Neither seemed aware of passing time until Raven breathed, 'Well, my girl, there's nothing you can do about it – you're in. So you're the one who needs to be careful.' And they smiled, both of them.

*

Telford looked across the cabin as he shrugged himself into his anorak. The Professor seemed to be tracking the boy and Naomi through the system, punching up monitor after monitor as they made their way through from cave to cave. Telford grunted farewell to the old man but got no reply as he slammed the cabin door behind him.

*

Raven drew a shape on the cave wall with a small piece of rock. 'It looked like the top half of a man. There's his head and arms, see… with a cross underneath.' He completed the symbol and Naomi stared at it in surprise.

'You've never seen that before?' She had to establish first whether or not this was some abstruse practical joke of Raven's but his look convinced her when he shook his head negatively. He was too concerned by the entire experience, she decided, to lie about any part of it. She traced the shape with her finger. 'It's the astrological symbol for Pluto.'

Raven was genuinely surprised. 'Pluto? That's a planet, right?'

Naomi nodded. 'A relatively newly discovered planet that does not appear in zodiacal symbolism to any great extent, yet. But it is supposed that it rules the newest form of power. Atomic energy.'

Raven couldn't keep the excitement out of his voice as he followed her idea. 'Pluto… plutonium…?'

Naomi was very serious. 'Exactly,' she muttered.

*

The Professor was tight in on the symbol. It loomed large on the monitor screen and he regarded it thoughtfully as he listened to Raven and Naomi discuss it. Mrs Young burst into the cabin and the confined space was suddenly alive with her manic energy as she tossed her clipboard and binoculars aside. 'Splendid! Two twites, four crossbills and a lesser redpoll. That makes sixteen redpoll sightings since the beginning of the year.' She crossed to stand behind the Professor. 'I'm going home, dear. Do you want to wait for Raven?'

The Professor continued to stare at Raven and Naomi on the monitor. 'No, no, he's got work to do.'

Really, thought his wife, there are times when he overplays the enigmatic bit. She watched the two young people on the screen. 'That young girl, he seems rather taken with her.'

'Yes,' breathed the Professor, softly.

Mrs Young became interested, despite the excitement of wanting to get home to log her sightings. 'What exactly are they doing?' she demanded.

The Professor hit several buttons in sequence and the entire apparatus died. He spun his chair to face his wife and searched her face to see if her question was merely an idle one. He decided that she actually needed an answer this time. 'Working things out,' was all he offered.

She manoeuvred him out of the cabin and down the ramp towards the car. 'It must be very gratifying for you, James, that you've managed to get him so interested.'

They struggled to get him out of the chair and into the passenger seat. Mrs Young folded the wheelchair and managed it into the back of the estate. She did not hear her husband's reply. She was thinking of what she had in the larder for his lunch.

The Professor stared out at the stone circle and said, 'Yes, he's being a great help.' Then, his hands arranging his useless legs into place, he thought, *I don't know what I'd have done without him.*

*

They reached the part of the system that they had set out to inspect. They were drawn in the right direction by the noise of the drills.

Naomi stopped dead and worriedly her hand grabbed Raven's shoulder. Shouting above the scream of the metal on rock, she yelled in the boy's ear, 'They can't do that.' She pointed to the symbol above the cave entrance. 'They are trying to drill through from Cancer to Capricorn.'

Raven looked at her as if she had taken leave of her senses. These were professionals, and they knew what they were doing.

She was white with worry. 'Connect Cancer to Capricorn... sure disaster,' she screamed.

Raven shrugged his shoulders questioningly and she dragged him away to a quieter place. Naomi still had to use full volume but it was easier on the ear. 'They're in opposition. Directly opposite each other in the Zodiac... an Earth sign and a Water sign. Earth suppresses Water and Water erodes Earth.' She was serious, and almost frantic in her concern.

Raven grinned. This was the point at which an interest in a harmless branch of a pseudo-science stopped being a bit of fun and started to become a nuisance. 'Better tell Bill, then. Go on, I dare you. Tell him to stop the tunnelling. That's what they're doing – test boring for a tunnel.'

Naomi froze and shook her head helplessly. 'Someone has to warn them.' She started to move back the way they had come, fast.

Raven grabbed her arm. Suddenly the fun went out of his voice, too. 'You're serious, aren't you? Really serious…?'

She spun before him and yelled urgently, 'Listen, Raven – there's no doubt this is a zodiac. Heaven alone knows where the twelfth cave is but it must be here somewhere. So if they're going to mess about with the system, they'd better know what they are doing.' She tore herself free and hustled through into the next cave, heading for the lift shaft.

Raven looked about him with renewed interest. 'Arthur's Round Table? Maybe this is where he found the energy to win all those battles…'

*

The Mini sped through the countryside, towards the old church, taking Mrs Young and the Professor back to the house for lunch. The rusty old wreck did its best as it climbed the hill but it was puffing a bit as it breasted the rise.

In the churchyard, a young, long-haired man in a garish teeshirt and blue jeans was mowing a neglected corner with a scythe. He looked up as the car approached and took the breather as an opportunity to sharpen the blade with the worn stone.

In the car, the Professor glanced at the young man sharpening his scythe and something in his stance and in the picture that he made in the dappled sunlight of the churchyard switched on some memory trace that the old man did not know existed. For a moment, he seemed to be in a trance; then, pulling himself together, he cried, 'Stop!'

His wife, far away in thoughts of her own, was startled into doing as she was bid. It was most unlike him to take decisions of this sort – she wondered what had gone wrong. It was obviously of some importance. The car protested to a halt.

The old man seemed almost frightened. 'Turn. Turn the car. Quick. Back to the site – now – quickly.'

She missed the gear in her anxiety to comply with these directions and the car backed into a field gateway and went back the way it had come.

*

Bill Telford stared down at Naomi's worried face with incredulous contempt. 'Look, Miss Grant,' he snapped impatiently. 'You may be very attractive and maybe you're God's gift to Fleet Street but I don't tell you how to do your job, so don't you tell me how to do mine. OK?'

'I'm not telling you how to do your job, Mr Telford,' she protested. 'But there's more to those caves than you know.'

Raven cut in. 'Listen to her, Bill. She's an expert.'

The big construction man whirled on the boy. 'Oh really? Got a degree in geology, either of you? Perhaps you'd like to study the report – give me your expert opinion?'

'It's nothing to do with geology.' Naomi practically

stamped her foot at him. 'You're connecting two caves that were never meant to be directly connected. There could be an accident.' As she said it, she realised how unconvincing her explanation was to this hard-headed man.

He exploded. 'You think we didn't do our homework? Every stratum of that rock has been tested and analysed. It's mainly granite and quartz, so it's ideal for tunnelling.'

'*No!*' Her vehemence shocked even Raven.

Telford glanced from the girl to the boy and back again. 'What do you mean, no?' he asked, despairingly, reasonably.

Naomi had run out of steam. She knew that she would never be able to convince him with her argument. Slowly, quietly, she pleaded, 'The place where you are tunnelling at the moment, you should stop before it is too late.'

The construction man waited to hear if there was any further explanation but Naomi hung her head. 'Just do me a favour, will you? Keep your pretty nose out of my business.'

Naomi raised her head and she was on the verge of tears. She stared at him hard for a moment, then turned away. 'Come on, Raven.'

The boy grinned up at the big man and shook his head sadly. 'I'm surprised at you, mate – I really am. A bloke with all your experience and no idea how to handle women – pathetic.'

Telford had had enough. 'Maybe not but I've an idea how to handle you…'

Raven dropped into an easy position, realising that he'd hit the nerve, that the man had had a bad day and that he was overmatched completely. 'Some other time, Bill. My karate's a bit rusty at the moment.'

The situation had got completely out of hand. Telford turned and stalked away. Raven watched him go until Naomi returned to his shoulder.

'Want a lift back?'

Raven shook his head. He was disappointed in his big friend, he felt that he had to put the situation on a better footing and yet make him see that the girl was serious in her estimate. 'No thanks, I'll stick around.'

She went and Raven watched her go, feeling more ill at ease by the moment. There was something in the wind, some storm brewing in his blood – he could feel it. Telford stood a few yards away suddenly and kicked at a loose rock. He looked like a large embarrassed schoolboy who realised that he had gone too far.

'You really believe that stuff?' he called. 'Or is it just because you fancy her?'

Raven went nearer, just a pace or two. 'She sounded pretty convincing...'

There was a long silence. There was nothing more to say now that peace had been made. 'I thought you had your head screwed on,' Bill jeered at his young friend.

Raven shuffled his feet, embarrassed at his own feelings, but something in Bill's tone made him go on. 'Yeah, well... it's true. I do fancy her.'

Telford did not move but he said, rather wistfully, 'Don't blame you. Listen, we're the same sort of blokes, you and me. We shouldn't be on opposite sides. Who changed your mind? The Prof?'

Raven nodded. 'He just explained a few things. Things I didn't understand before... but surely that doesn't mean we've got to stop being mates, does it?'

He studied the big man's face until it broke into its normal friendly grin. 'I've got to do the rounds. Coming?'

Raven grinned back. All was well.

*

Naomi sat typing but her mind was not focused on the words on the paper. She was thoughtful and preoccupied, her mind still troubled by her premonition of the disaster she was sure would happen in the caves if the drilling continued.

The Editor entered and hurried across the office towards his booth. Naomi stopped typing and called him over. He stood, looking down at her, waiting as patiently as he could for her to sort out her head.

'What do you know about Pluto?' The question surprised him, even coming from his favourite lunatic...

'Pluto?' He stalled, wondering what her next move might be. 'Not much. Belonged to Mickey Mouse, of course. Fond of bones...'

'Not the dog. The planet.'

'Ah.' Rather less good on this one, he thought. 'Discovered about 1930, I believe. Named after the god of the Underworld?'

Naomi nodded, pleased. 'Right. And represented astrologically by this symbol.' She held up a sheet of paper on which she had drawn the symbol that Raven had shown her.

Her boss shrugged, 'So...?'

She explained Raven's experience in the so-called gas pocket and the significance of the symbol in his story.

The Editor smiled. 'Fascinating. "Boy Sees Vision In

Cave". Anything further, Scoop?' He moved as if to go to his own office.

Naomi jumped ahead quickly. 'The point is, he had no idea what the symbol signified. He'd never seen it before.'

Her editor kept going, calling back over his shoulder, 'How do you know? He probably found out you were into the prediction business and did a bit of homework.'

Naomi followed him, grabbing a large volume from beside her typewriter. 'Why should he do that?' She was puzzled by his cynicism.

'The way to an astrologer's heart is through her symbols.'

The man was infuriating. 'All that trouble just to chat me up? He's not that devious. Anyway, it's odd that he should have chosen this particular sign. Pluto governs change; it has the power to turn lazy, selfish lives into happy, constructive ones. Under its influence, people discover a sense of purpose.' She paused to see what effect, if any, her words were having.

The head was shaking slowly from side to side. 'Oh, come on, Naomi. You believe what you want to believe but don't expect me to swallow your codswallop. Your predecessor was every bit as accurate in his predictions – and he used a pin.'

'Taurus!' snapped the girl. 'You're just what I'd expect of a Taurean. Stubborn and cynical.'

'Or hardheaded and realistic.'

'Call it what you like but there's a story here, with an unusual angle.'

Why would he not see the obvious? She gave up and turned for the door but he blew smoke towards her as he lit his cigarette and said, 'Try me…' He was grinning at her hotheadness as she turned back to face him.

'This is King Arthur country, right?'

'According to the British Tourist Authority.' He broke the match between his fingers.

Naomi opened the book she had been cradling in her arms. 'Listen to this. "At the battle of Camlann, Arthur received a mortal blow from his nephew, Mordred. He was then carried in a boat to the Isle of Avalon, where his wound was healed. So the great King did not die but rests in slumber with his knights until such time as he is needed again…" ' She looked up. He was still staring at her but his smile had been replaced by a look of gathering interest.

Naomi started to repeat a segment, with emphasis. ' "So the great King did not die but rests in slumber…" '

He shook his head sadly: she had missed the point. 'And you are relating this to that young tearaway?'

'I told you it had an unusual angle.' She believed the angle, she really did – he could see that she was now committed to possibility.

'Unusual? It's ridiculous.' But he knew that he was not going to shake her conviction.

She slammed the book down on the desk. 'It'll sell copies!' She knew she was right and he knew that she had the glimmer of a chance.

He paced around the desk and back out into the main office, heading for her desk. Naomi tucked into his shadow and followed as closely as she could whilst avoiding the cigarette smoke that wreathed about him. ' "Young King Returns to Fight Infidel". Yes, I suppose it has possibilities. All right, see what you can do. If it's any good, we'll run it.'

Her heart leaped and she took the cigarette from between his lips and kissed him heartily. Just the chance, that's all she had asked. She grabbed her bag and ran across the office, leaving him at her desk wondering what was happening now. 'I've got to get back to the site,' she called and she was gone.

Left to himself, he stole a glance at the copy in her typewriter – it wasn't bad – and then he smiled, and said aloud, 'I wonder if Guinevere fancied herself as a reporter?' But by now she was out of earshot.

*

The shift had finished, and the workers of both parties were gone as Bill and Raven climbed into protective suits and helmets at the head of the lift shaft.

Raven asked, 'So what will you do if Naomi's prediction is right?'

Bill grinned. 'Resign.'

'You'd take it that personally?'

The big man stepped into the lift and closed the gates. 'No. But the management might.' He hit the down button. 'Anyway, tunnelling's almost through. Tomorrow'll see it complete.'

*

The Professor watched the monitor bank closely. He punched up the cave where the tunnelling had been taking place. The machinery stood silent and deserted.

Naomi knocked and entered at the cabin door. The old man did not turn but merely said, 'Come in, Miss Grant.' She stood behind him and tried to see what it was that was interesting him so much.

Disbelieving her own eyes, she felt her fingers tighten into the Professor's shoulder as the Pluto symbol began to form on the monitor screen.

'Look... just as Raven said... the sign of Pluto...' She could not keep the wonder out of her unsteady voice.

The Professor nodded, smiling enigmatically up at her. But behind the smile there was another sense. She tried to read what it was until she realised that the only thing that she could see in the old man's eyes was the reflection of the sign of Pluto...

*

Raven and Telford moved easily through the cave system. Suddenly a sound made them both freeze – footsteps, distant laughter, the jingling of horse harness, a haunting strain of music...

*

On the monitor, the Professor and Naomi watched as Raven and Telford moved tentatively forward. On other monitors, strange shapes ghosted across the screens. Raven's voice came hoarsely from the system.

'Those were the sounds I heard.'

Telford changed direction, casting about for a centre to the sound. 'This way.'

Raven and Telford appeared on another monitor as they passed into a further cave.

Naomi spoke low, urgently, to the Professor. 'Warn them, Professor, tell them...'

He reached forward and covered the talkback

microphone with his hand. He was still smiling quietly to himself. 'Wait.'

His confidence calmed Naomi for a moment but her heart beat so loudly that it was almost the only thing of which she was aware.

*

Raven and Telford listened. The sounds continued but always in the next cave, always around the next corner.

Bill glanced at his young colleague. He could feel the fear in the boy. Partly to give himself confidence he called, 'Who's there?'

There... ere... ere... echoed back. There was no other answer. They both became aware that the odd thing about the sounds that they could hear was that there was no echo caused by them.

Telford grabbed Raven's arm and headed back towards the cave where the tunnelling equipment lay.

On the monitor, Telford and the boy entered the cave and looked about. Suddenly all the sounds and the ghosting on the screens had stopped.

Bill yelled, 'Is there anyone left down here?'

And there was silence, apart from the echoes of his voice.

Raven moved to the mouth of the tunnel and peered in. Expecting blackness, he was chilled by the sight he saw.

'Bill!' he called to his friend, in warning.

In the tunnel, the Pluto sign was forming in mid-air. Telford moved to Raven's side. As though hypnotised, he walked forward, drawn into the tunnel by the power of the symbol. Figures started to ghost about Telford's body as he moved calmly forward. Faces that Raven had seen in his vision became clear again... the music reached the sweetness of climax...

Raven shook himself into action. 'No, Bill... don't! Come back!' He leaped after his friend as he heard from above them a rumbling sound... a cracking of the tunnel walls, the sound of rock in movement as the cave started to collapse.

Chapter Seven

UP IN THE PORTAKABIN, NAOMI was staring at the monitor screen with horrified disbelief. From the mouth of the tunnel came a small avalanche of rubble, accompanied by a cloud of dust which gradually blinded the camera's eye. The Professor flicked a switch and the cabin was suddenly full of sound – a low rumbling growl, as if the earth was rebelling against the torture it was suffering at the hands of man. A giant, provoked beyond endurance, turning in fury on his persecutors.

It was terrible. Impossible to believe that Bill and Raven were somewhere in that dust fog, crushed under the fallen rock. Naomi had been sure that trouble was brewing, but she had been quite unprepared for such an appalling tragedy.

She remained motionless, transfixed by the screen. 'No!' she whispered. Then, with rising panic, 'No, no, *no!*'

The Professor was hunched in front of the control panel,

his face an expressionless mask. How could he just sit there? Perhaps he was too numb with shock to think clearly.

She grabbed him by the shoulder and swung him round to face her. He looked perfectly calm: almost... content. As if everything was as it should be. And when he spoke, there was not a trace of urgency in his voice.

'52311,' he said. 'That's the Emergency Service number.'

Naomi turned, picked up the phone and started to dial, stabbing her finger savagely into the holes.

'Hullo,' said a voice.

'Rockfall in the caves. Two people buried. Hurry.' She banged down the receiver and spun round, just as the dust cloud on the monitor began to clear. And out of the hazy background, a dark shape materialised, stumbling towards the camera – a dishevelled phantom that she didn't immediately recognise.

But the voice was unmistakeable. 'Professor!' it called. 'Naomi! Can you hear me?' The figure bent double, overcome by a sudden bout of coughing.

Naomi stifled a little sob of relief and rushed forward to yell into the Professor's ear. 'Go on. Answer him.'

The Professor switched on the talkback. 'We hear you, Raven.'

'Bill's in the tunnel. Under all that – all that...' Raven stood in front of the lens, his shoulders heaving, fighting for breath. Particles of dust were still floating in the air, and he clamped a handkerchief over his mouth.

Naomi leant forward and called to him. 'It's okay, Raven. We saw it all. A rescue team's on its way.'

Raven still looked dazed. 'I'm going back in there. See if

there's anything I can do.'

'No.' Naomi fought to keep the shrillness out of her voice. 'Please – don't move. Stay exactly where you are. Stay where we can see you. Everything's under control.'

'Under control? With Bill buried under all that rock?'

'Leave it to the professionals. They'll be here any minute.'

'That's not soon enough. He needs help now.' Raven turned, and started to move away from the camera.

Naomi shouted after him. 'Stop. There's nothing you can do. Raven!' But he took no notice, stumbling off in the direction of the tunnel.

The Professor flicked switch after switch, following his progress from cave to cave. Naomi watched with mounting alarm. 'We've got to stop him. There might be another fall.'

The Professor remained irritatingly calm. 'Follow your own advice, my dear. Leave it to the professionals.'

'But they may be too late. I'm going down.'

She rushed to the door, but the Professor held up a restraining hand. 'Listen.'

Hand on the doorknob, Naomi listened. The plaintive wail of an approaching siren was music to her ears. She wrenched the door open, just as a Land Rover swung in to the construction site, the orange light on its roof flashing like a friendly beacon. It skidded to a halt a few yards away, and half a dozen men jumped down. A young man in a green anorak who seemed to be their leader appeared out of the driving seat and barked at them.

'Get the gear out. Quick as you can.' He strode over to the Portakabin, and nodded to Naomi.

'You the young lady who phoned?'

'Yes.'

'Two people buried, you say?'

'One's safe. He's still down there, though.'

'Right. Let's have a look at the plan.'

He brushed past her into the cabin. The Professor already had the plan spread out on the control panel. He looked up and found himself face to face with the young man from the churchyard. 'Eleven minutes. You've been quick,' he said glancing at the clock.

'Not quick enough.' The young man sounded reassuringly experienced. 'If I'd had more practice with this team, we'd have done it in half the time. Now – where's the fall?'

'Here.' The Professor's finger stabbed at the chart. 'The boy – Raven – he's safe enough. The other – Bill Telford, the site manager – is still somewhere in the tunnel.'

'What tunnel?'

'Between these two caves. They were trying to connect them by drilling through the central core.'

'You mean, it was the drilling that caused the fall?'

'No.' Naomi moved to stand by the young man's side. 'They weren't drilling at the time. It just – collapsed.'

'For no apparent reason?'

'I can think of a reason. But it doesn't matter now.'

The young man picked up the plan and folded it. 'Sounds as if someone hasn't done his homework. Where's the lift shaft?'

'I'll show you.' She turned and led the way out of the cabin.

*

Down below, Raven picked his way over piles of rubble to the blocked tunnel. After the roar of the rockfall, the caves were eerily quiet. It was as if they were brooding, waiting for the intruder's response to the recent demonstration of their power.

The air was still thick with dust, and Raven kept the handkerchief pressed tightly over his mouth. With his free hand, he picked up a small stone and banged it on one of the huge rocks that filled the tunnel entrance. The chinking sound echoed away into the recesses of the cave system, and then the silence returned once more, heavy with menace. Raven had the uneasy feeling that at any moment the place might decide to bury him as well. He couldn't explain it – he knew it was impossible – but he was suddenly convinced that this intricate geological network had a mind of its own.

He banged on the rock again and called. 'Bill…?' His voice ricocheted off the walls, and he could hear the hopelessness in it. Could there still be life behind that solid mass? The odds against it were long, and getting longer with every passing minute.

Naomi had said the rescue team was on its way, but what could they do in the face of such an obstacle? They probably wouldn't have the necessary equipment, and even after it arrived it would take them hours to cut through the rock. Rescuing trapped potholers was no preparation for an accident on this scale.

He bent down and scrabbled desperately at some of the smaller rocks, flinging them behind him with primitive savagery. If the caves wanted a fight, they could have one. He wouldn't give up until he was certain that Bill was dead.

Somewhere in the distance, he heard the lift gates clang.

He took no notice, working with cold fury at the barrier that separated him from his friend. But it was a losing battle. The more debris he cleared away, the more fell down to take its place. Tortured by aching muscles, he collapsed to his knees in exhaustion and despair.

Naomi and the young man appeared, followed by the rest of the team carrying a heavy drill. Seeing Raven, Naomi gave a gasp of relief: then ran forward and helped him to his feet.

Raven staggered a little. 'In there,' he muttered weakly. 'Bill's somewhere in there.'

'I know.' Naomi dragged him away from the rockface. 'The men are here now. Leave it to them.'

He tried to shake her off. 'Still alive. I know he's still alive…'

'Quiet!' The young man had produced an instrument that looked like a doctor's stethoscope. 'I must have absolute silence.'

'Come on,' said Naomi, tugging at Raven's arm. 'We'll only be in the way.'

The young man peeled off his anorak. 'Trust me, Raven. It's my job, saving people.' He turned, to reveal a vicar's dog-collar under his sports jacket.

Raven stared at him in astonishment. 'Yeah. I suppose it is. Not usually this far down though, are you?'

The vicar smiled and hung the listening device round his neck. 'At your age, I was a veteran potholer. So I divided my loyalties between heaven and – down here. How far in is he?'

Raven shrugged. 'Dunno.'

The vicar unfolded the plan of the caves and beckoned

to him. 'We're here,' he said, pointing, 'and here's the two caves they were trying to connect. How far had they got with the tunnel?'

'About half-way. And Bill was standing near the face when the roof fell in. Must be about there.'

'Got it.' The vicar studied the chart closely. 'Could be up to fifteen feet of blockage. Anything more, and he won't stand a chance.'

Raven looked at him in horror. 'You've got to get through to him – you've just got to.' He grabbed the lapels of the vicar's jacket, pulled him towards him and stared into his face, wild-eyed.

The vicar gently disentangled himself. 'We'll do everything we can. Has there been any sound?'

'No.'

'You've shouted? Called his name?'

'I've shouted… banged… knocked. Not a whisper.'

'Right. Let's try the scientific approach.'

He moved to the rockface, placed the headset of the listening device over his ears and held the miniature microphone against the rubble, listening intently. Raven and Naomi watched him anxiously, nerves tingling.

The vicar took off his headset and turned to the waiting men. 'Nothing. Get the drill set up.' As the rest of the team carried the drill into position, he moved back to Raven and put a comforting hand on his shoulder. 'Best thing you can do is rest. You won't do any good by hanging around here.'

Raven nodded, and allowed Naomi to take his arm and lead him out of the cave. Behind them, the drill clattered into life, shattering the silence with a deafening whine.

Raven stopped and closed his eyes. The strain of the last

half-hour had taken its toll, and he suddenly felt at the end of his resources. He had nothing left, either mentally or physically.

When he opened his eyes again, he saw that Naomi was staring with awestruck reverence at the entrance to the next cave.

A man was leaning against the wall, immediately below the Gemini symbol. He was tall and handsome, with a face that Raven vaguely recognised – though he couldn't remember where he had seen him before. The man had his hands in his pockets, and was regarding them with languid nonchalance, as if he was out for an afternoon stroll and had stopped to admire the view.

'Hello, loveys,' he said. 'I seem to be lost. Could you point me in the direction of the pulsating subterranean drama?'

Naomi continued to regard him as if he were a creature from another planet. 'You mean the rockfall?' She waved towards the Cancer cave. 'Through there.'

'Ta ever so.' The man favoured them with a lazy smile, detached himself from the wall, and sauntered unhurriedly past them.

Raven was puzzled. The stranger seemed to know all about the accident, yet was apparently untouched by it. How could anyone remain so calm while Bill's life hung in the balance?

He called after him. 'Hey. You part of the rescue team?'

The man turned to gaze at him with piercing blue eyes. 'You talking to me?'

Raven felt Naomi's elbow digging into his ribs. 'Don't be silly, Raven,' she said. 'Everyone knows Clive Castle.'

'Please.' Castle looked away and winced. 'No time for teenage adulation. Got work to do.'

'What sort of work?' asked Raven.

Naomi nudged him again. '*Today People*. On the telly.'

So that's who he was. The 'Clive Castle Show' was one of the programmes they had been allowed to see at Ferndown, because the Governor thought it was important for the lads to keep in touch with current affairs. The prospect of watching a bunch of politicians explaining why they were making a mess of the country had made them groan with boredom, but Raven had found to his surprise that week after week the show consistently held his interest.

And the reason was Castle himself – the front man who didn't let his guests get away with anything. The questions he asked were intelligent and penetrating, and the moment anyone began to waffle and become evasive he pounced like a panther. It was fun watching his prey squirm and wriggle, and those razor-sharp teeth biting deeper and deeper. It was a wonder so many important people agreed to appear on the show, because not one of them came out of it unscathed. It wasn't as if they didn't know what they were in for.

Women seemed to swarm round Castle like bees. He was always in the papers with a girl on each arm, and six months ago Raven had read an article which named him as 'Britain's Most Eligible Bachelor'. Even Naomi seemed to have been knocked sideways by his charm, like a teeny-bopper who had suddenly come face to face with a rock star.

He decided to snap her out of it, bring her back to her senses. If he could make her laugh, surely she would realise she was behaving like a schoolkid? And he was good at making people laugh.

He moved forward and peered into the man's face. 'Clive Castle, eh? Hey, you're right. I thought he was just a talking head.'

The blue eyes looked ice-cold. 'I am. I hire the body specially for outside broadcasts.' He giggled, hugely pleased with this comeback, and Raven had to admit that it was pretty sharp. It was no use trying to engage this sophisticated man-of-the-world in a verbal battle: he'd had far too much practice.

Naomi turned and looked up at the camera in the corner of the cave. 'Professor?' she called.

The Professor's amplified voice boomed down at them. 'Yes, my dear?'

'Clive Castle's here.'

'Yes, I know. He's an old friend. Welcome, Mr Castle.'

'Thank you, Professor.' Castle gazed up at the camera as if he could see the Professor himself, crouched on a ledge above him. Raven noticed that when he addressed the disembodied voice, he spoke with deference. He seemed to treat the deep tones that reverberated round the cave as reverently as Naomi had treated him.

But when he finally looked away from the camera, all his lazy arrogance had returned. 'Come on,' he said. 'Let's go and find that poor unfortunate chappie.'

Naomi nodded and led the way back towards the tunnel.

The drill's ear-splitting clatter stopped suddenly as they re-entered the Cancer cave. The vicar motioned them to remain silent as one of his team picked up the headset and held the microphone to the small hole they had bored through the rock.

The headset man listened intently for a moment… frowned… then moved the microphone slowly round the hole, like a doctor exploring a patient's pain-area. He turned and beckoned to the vicar to take his place.

The vicar went through the same routine and reacted with brisk urgency. 'Yes. No question. Some sort of movement.'

Raven rushed up, and grabbed him by the shoulder. 'He's alive?'

The vicar waved at his colleagues and issued a curt command. 'Try for response,' then, to Raven, 'We'll send an intermittent signal. See if he can answer.'

The men opened an electronic box of tricks, attached the wires to the rock and began to transmit a *beep-beep* signal. Raven glanced round, noticed a spare headset lying in a corner and picked it up, indicating to the vicar that he too wanted to listen. The vicar smiled and switched it on for him. They stood side by side at the rockface, waiting. Raven held his breath.

Beep-beep… ten seconds' silence… *beep-beep*. The signals pulsed through the rock like a slow heartbeat. The pauses between them were agonisingly empty, and hope began to wither. He glanced round at Naomi and Castle standing by the cave entrance and shrugged. Naomi gave him a wan smile of encouragement, but it was only a mask: tense expectancy was rapidly giving way to despair.

And then – deep in the recesses of the blocked tunnel – the faint *chip-chip* of rock on rock. Raven froze. An echo of their own signal? No, there it was again, slightly louder. And again…

He turned to the vicar, electrified with excitement. 'That's him! He's alive…'

'Quiet.' The vicar snapped at his team. 'Use the stethoscope to get a siting. Three positions, then cross-refer to get an exact fix.'

Raven took off his headset and bellowed at the rock. 'Bill!'

The vicar put an understanding hand on his shoulder. 'It's too soon for that,' he said. 'We're still too far away. Now clear off and leave it to the experts. We'll let you know when we get close enough for voice contact.'

Raven stepped aside as the rescue team went to work, taking detailed soundings. He stood watching them for a moment, then turned towards the entrance to find that Naomi and Castle were no longer there.

He wandered out, back towards the lift shaft, and found the Aries cave filled with men and equipment. A construction gang was carrying a massive piece of machinery out of the lift, while two or three trendily dressed strangers unpacked a television camera, watched by Castle.

'It's the story of the year, Max,' he was saying. 'And we're clever enough to be on the spot, waiting for it to unfold. So if you've forgotten to bring any film I shall be just the teensiest bit cross.'

Max glanced up and inspected the cave's spotlights with a professional eye. 'I've plenty of film, Clive,' he said sourly, 'but you can't expect me to win any Academy Awards in this gloom.'

Castle grinned. 'Make do and mend – a true artist should always be able to improvise. I mean, if we had full studio lighting down here, you'd waste valuable time making your barn doors Chinese, and putting half-blues in your inky-dinks.'

Raven frowned. He supposed television crews were used to disasters, but this callous disregard for human life upset him. Didn't they care whether Bill was rescued or not? It seemed that nothing mattered to this lot except their flaming lighting.

'What are we going to do?' asked Max. 'Use the handheld?'

'No, I think we can do better than that,' said Castle. 'I'll talk to the old boy up in the cabin. I'm pretty sure we can detach one of his cameras and use the terminal for ours.'

Max nodded, and he and the other trendies lifted the camera onto its stand. Castle watched them with approval. 'There's a working priest in charge of the operation,' he said dreamily. 'Not just a pretty cassock. I can't wait to immortalise him.'

Raven turned away in disgust, just as Naomi moved up to him. She indicated the huge piece of equipment which the construction men were carrying off in the direction of the tunnel. 'Heavy drill,' she said. 'That should speed things up.'

They followed the men back into the Taurus cave.

*

Up in the Portakabin, the Professor sat in front of the bank of monitors, his eyes flicking from screen to screen. By means of his electronic eyes, he had followed every step of the rescue operation, and had been impressed by the way Raven had handled himself. Yes, the boy was coming on well: as he had expected, the tragedy was having a remarkable effect on him. The boy was turning into a man.

The door opened and Mrs Young bustled in, carrying a basket of food and some thermos flasks. 'I came as soon as I could,' she said. 'What a terrible thing. But one of the men told me they think Mr Telford's safe, thank goodness.'

'There are signs of life, apparently.' The Professor watched with satisfaction as the construction men set to work with the heavy drill. 'I shouldn't worry. I'm sure they're going to get him out.'

Mrs Young set down the basket and stared at her husband curiously. 'I really don't know how you can stay so calm.'

The Professor smiled. 'When one's been a cripple as long as I have, one learns to accept one's own impotence.'

Raven's voice floated up from the caves. 'Prof? We've found him. He's alive.'

The Professor glanced at the Gemini monitor, and saw Raven give the thumbs-up sign towards the camera. He flicked the talkback switch. 'I know. I saw and heard it all. You've done well, Raven.'

Raven grinned. 'Nothing to do with me, guv. It was that bionic vicar.'

Mrs Young leaned over the Professor's shoulder. 'Hungry, Raven?'

'Starving.'

'Come and get it, then.'

'Great. I'll tell Madame Futura.' He moved off in the direction of the tunnel.

Mrs Young breathed a sigh of relief. 'Well, it doesn't seem to have affected his appetite. If he'd said he wasn't hungry, I'd have feared the worst.'

The Professor took her hand and looked up at her tenderly. 'I don't know what we'd all do without you, my dear.'

'Why? What have I done?'

'You chose the right boy. Out of all those young tearaways, you chose the right one. It was really very clever of you.'

She had no idea what he meant, but the warmth of his tone made her beam with pleasure.

*

The heavy drill made twice as much noise as the light one. The sound was amplified by the hollow ring of caves, and Raven stood below the Cancer symbol, deafened.

The vicar moved up to him and yelled in his ear. 'We've got a fix on him. He's about where you said he'd be.'

'Great,' Raven shouted back. 'How long do you reckon?'

'Hard to tell. There's about eight feet of solid garbage to get through. The trouble is, we've got a time-space equation, and I've been trying to work it out.'

'How d'you mean?'

'Well, if my calculations are correct, he's got about five or six feet of clear tunnel between the rockfall and the face.'

'A cosy little cell, eh?' Raven grinned. 'No worse than being in the nick.'

The vicar looked grave. 'He's got a problem that ordinary prisoners don't have.'

'What's that?'

'Air. At a rough guess, he's got about fifteen minutes' worth of oxygen left. If we don't get through to him by then, he'll have had it.'

Raven stared at him, aghast. 'But I thought we'd found him. I thought everything was going great.'

'Finding him's one thing – reaching him's another. And we're running out of time.'

Raven turned, to find Naomi standing by his side. She had overheard the vicar's last remark and was staring at him with saucer eyes. To their right, Castle was waving his camera crew nearer to the rockface, seemingly oblivious to the seriousness of the situation. The pounding of the drill filled Raven's mind and numbed his senses with thunder.

Chapter Eight

THEY SAT AROUND THE PORTAKABIN, attacking the chicken legs that Mrs Young had brought in her basket. Raven and Naomi were eating to kill time, but Castle was tucking in with relish.

'What a mouth-watering repast, madam,' he said, as Mrs Young filled his paper plate with ham and tongue and paté, 'and how you managed to rustle it up at such short notice is a mystery. It's a cold collation worthy of the Savoy.'

Mrs Young simpered. Raven stopped gnawing his chicken-leg and stared at her in surprise. So she, too, was impressed by this tall, effeminate bag of wind. It was unbelievable. Couldn't any of these women see that underneath his fancy talk there was nothing but self-importance and conceit? There was only one word for him – *yuk*!

The Professor sat motionless in front of the monitors, his eyes glued to the master screen. Castle's crew had attached their lead to the cave-camera terminal, so that the pictures they were now receiving in the cabin had all the movement and excitement of live television.

Down below, the vicar and his rescue team stood watching the construction men boring into the rock with the heavy drill. They were making some progress, but it was hard going.

Raven glanced at the clock. The time seemed to be rushing by, but he saw that only five minutes had passed since the vicar had warned him that Bill was running out of air.

Ten minutes left: would they make it? They'd cut about a foot into the rock, and if the vicar's figures were right they still had another seven feet to go. So if they kept up the same drilling rate – a foot every five minutes – it would be more than half an hour before they were through. And that would be too late! Infuriated by his utter helplessness, Raven threw his chicken-leg across the cabin. By some curious chance, it hit the plan of the caves hanging on the opposite wall and left a dark stain at exactly the spot where the men were tunnelling.

He felt Mrs Young's hand on his shoulder. 'Eat, Raven. Have some cheese. It's good for shock.'

Her unspoken sympathy made his eyes smart. Ashamed of his sudden weakness, he stuffed a hunk of cheese into his mouth and nodded his gratitude.

Castle, however, remained completely unsympathetic: he seemed to believe that the accident had been staged for his benefit, and that the outcome didn't really matter.

'When they get through, Raven,' he said, spooning some potato salad into his mouth, 'I want you to be the first to talk to him.'

Raven gritted his teeth. 'Just try and stop me.'

'That's the spirit. It'll make a great opening for the programme.'

This was too much, even for Naomi. 'Only if there's a happy ending,' she reminded him.

Castle turned to her with raised eyebrows. 'There's no reason to doubt that, is there?'

Raven opened his mouth to tell him about the vicar's grim prediction, but the Professor spoke first. 'Tell him, Miss Grant. Tell him about your – premonition.'

Castle favoured her with a dazzling smile. 'Well?'

'I warned Bill,' said Naomi softly. 'Tunnelling between those two caves was asking for trouble.'

'Why?'

'Cancer and Capricorn. They're in opposition.'

Castle looked puzzled. 'Explain.'

'This cave system forms a terrestrial zodiac. I knew it'd be dangerous to join Cancer and Capricorn, because it's the same with people. Some signs get on with each other, and some don't. What are you, Mr Castle?'

'Me? I'm Gemini.'

'The first air sign. And I'm Libra – another air sign. That's why we're likely to hit it off. But put Cancer and Capricorn together, and there are bound to be fireworks.'

Castle turned to the Professor. 'Is she serious?'

'Not only serious, but right.'

Castle frowned, obviously taken aback that the renowned archaeologist seemed to swallow such rubbish without question. And Raven could see that he was re-examining the theory in the light of the Professor's answer. There was no doubt that the respect with which he treated the old man was genuine.

For Raven, it was Castle's only redeeming feature. He found himself disliking that pale, finely chiselled face more and more, and wondered what it would look like with a broken nose and a black eye. And perhaps a cracked rib or two as well: someone ought to teach him what suffering was all about.

He couldn't understand Naomi. A level-headed girl like that, turning into a zombie just because she'd seen him on the telly – it made you sick. He was bitterly disappointed in her; in the fact that, intelligent as she was, she couldn't see through someone so transparently worthless.

Yet she'd been clever enough to predict this disaster: all that stuff about Cancer and Capricorn had been spot on. So why couldn't she use her astrological knowledge to rescue Bill? If Cancer didn't go with Capricorn, what did it go with? It was a long shot, but it was better than just sitting around, doing nothing.

He ran to the control panel, leaned across the Professor and turned up the sound from below, flooding the cabin with instant uproar... the humming of the generator, the pumping of the compressor, and above them both, the screaming of the drill. The Professor glanced up at him and shrugged: they would never make themselves heard over such a pandemonium.

Raven hit the talkback switch and yelled into the microphone. '*Vicar!*' The vicar took no notice. He shouted into the Professor's ear. 'What's his name?'

The Professor picked up a pencil and wrote on a notepad. *Wakefield.*

Raven bellowed into the mike again. '*Wakefield!*'

The vicar turned, hesitated, then moved out into the Gemini cave and looked enquiringly up at the camera.

The Professor punched up the picture on the main monitor and flicked another switch, reducing the noise to a bearable level. Then, indicating the appropriate talkback, he gestured to Raven to go ahead.

Raven bent down towards the mike. 'How's it going?'

The vicar shrugged. 'Slowly.'

'Getting close?'

'Not close enough.'

'How long?'

'Hard to tell. It's tough going.'

In the cave behind him, the whine of the drill suddenly changed pitch. A few seconds more, and the drilling stopped altogether. The vicar turned, disappeared into the Cancer cave and returned a moment later, looking dejected.

'What happened?' asked Raven.

'Another drill-bit gone. The third. We'll have to send for more.'

'But they won't arrive in time.'

The vicar nodded miserably. Raven switched off the talkback and turned to stare at the model of the cave system on Bill's desk.

The Professor wheeled his chair round to face him and gave him a challenging look. 'You have an idea?'

'Yeah.'

'Out with it, then. There's not much time.'

'Depends on Naomi.' Raven took Naomi's arm and led her over to the model. 'Look. Here's the tunnel. And here's where Bill's trapped – half-way between Cancer and Capricorn. Now what's this cave here?'

Naomi peered at the model. 'Aquarius.'

'Suppose we connected Aquarius and Cancer? Would that be good or bad?'

'Air and water? Good.'

'Right. That's got to be our way in.'

Mrs Young stared at him incredulously. 'You're talking about rock, dear, not people. And a horoscope won't cut through rock.'

'Yes, it will.' Naomi looked at Raven with a new respect. 'It's worth a try anyway.'

Castle had wandered up and was inspecting the model closely. 'But it's about twelve feet from the Aquarius cave to the end of the tunnel. How can it be easier to drill through twelve feet than through eight?'

Raven glanced round to find the Professor's eyes burning into him.

'Tell him, Prof.'

'Later!' The old man wheeled his chair back to the control panel and surveyed the bank of monitors. Seeing Stone, the geologist, standing with a group of construction men in the Taurus cave, he punched up the picture on the master screen and spoke urgently into the talkback.

'Mr Stone? I need you in the Portakabin. Quick as you can, please.'

Stone nodded. 'I was coming up anyway, Professor. We've got a real problem here.'

The Professor switched off the sound and turned back to Raven. 'He won't like it, you know.'

'Why not?'

'Because it's unscientific. And if it works, it'll make nonsense of his own report.'

'Tough.' Raven stared thoughtfully round the room, then strode over to a large cabinet. 'Here – you,' he said to Castle, enjoying his moment of authority, 'give us a hand.'

Castle threw up his hands in mock horror. 'With that beast of a thing? Better ask someone else. I'm absolutely hopeless at anything physical.'

Raven made no effort to hide his contempt. 'We don't have to lift it, just tip it forward.' The man was a complete drip – surely even Naomi could see it now?

'Well, all right. On your head be it.' Castle giggled at his little joke, grabbed the other side of the cabinet, and together they tilted it slowly forward.

'Now sideways,' said Raven.

Castle groaned. 'I hope there's method in your madness,' he grunted, red in the face from the strain of trying to keep the cabinet on an even keel.

Together, they manoeuvred their burden to one side, so that it was resting on one corner. Castle was making a hissing noise, like an overheated steam-engine, but it was Raven who was taking most of the weight. Not that he felt any strain: his young muscles had been conditioned by years of arduous physical training. And the fact that Naomi was watching made the heavy metal feel as light as a feather.

Supporting the cabinet on his chest, he leaned across Bill's desk and picked up a thin plastic ruler. He slipped it into the crack above the top drawer and grinned at Naomi. 'Give it a whack on the top.'

She frowned. 'Why?'

'Don't argue. Just do it.'

She banged the top of the cabinet with her fist. Nothing happened.

'Harder,' said Raven.

She banged again and the top drawer slid open. Mrs Young bent down and picked up the ruler. 'What a clever trick, Raven. You must teach me how to do it.'

Raven and Castle pushed the cabinet back into position. Castle took out a spotless white handkerchief and mopped the sweat off his forehead. 'If I die of a heart attack,' he warned darkly, 'I shall come back and haunt you.' But he, too, seemed impressed by Raven's expertise.

Raven searched quickly through the files in the open drawer, found the one he was looking for and carried it over to the Professor. 'Here we are, Prof. The survey.'

The Professor opened the file and leafed through a series of large-scale geological charts, spattered with strange, different-coloured symbols. Then he squinted up at Raven, shrewd, bright eyes under bushy eyebrows. 'Well? What do you want to know?'

'Those red marks. What do they mean?'

'They're places where they've done some test drilling.'

'What about the rock between Aquarius and Cancer? Have they made any tests there?'

The Professor turned to the relevant chart and pointed to it wordlessly. There were no red symbols in the area.

Raven turned to Naomi. 'No tests anywhere near. That's great.'

She looked bewildered. 'Why?'

''Cos they're only guessing that rock wall's solid. Could be made of peanut brittle for all we know.'

'Ah. So we might be able to get through there?'

'That's our game, anyway. We've got to con 'em into thinking they've missed out. Get 'em to make a test.'

Castle gave a contemptuous snort, and Raven was delighted to see that this irritated Naomi. Stupid berk! He'd never get anywhere with her if he started sending up her astrology. Maybe it was just a question of time – time for her to get the stars out of her eyes and see him for the snide toffee-nose he really was!

The Professor, who had been staring at the Cancer cave monitor, glanced round at Naomi. 'Isn't that a friend of yours?'

She frowned at the screen. 'Yes. The vultures are gathering, it seems.'

Raven followed her gaze, and saw the Editor standing near the tunnel entrance, chatting to the vicar. 'So he's heard. He can't be too pleased with you for not phoning in.'

Naomi shrugged. 'I gave him advance warning. Told him something was about to happen.'

Raven bent down and punched up the talkback. 'Wakefield?'

The vicar broke off his conversation and turned towards the camera. 'No news yet, Raven.'

Raven turned away from the control panel and glanced at the clock. Less than ten minutes before Bill's air ran out. 'Come on, Stone,' he muttered. 'What's keeping you?'

As if in answer to his prayer, the door opened and Stone appeared. His face was lined with fatigue, and he slumped wearily into a chair. 'We've got a potential strike on our hands,' he announced. 'Some of the construction men are beginning to believe the caves are under some sort of curse; that the rockfall and the gear failure were caused by some supernatural force. They're saying that after this rescue operation, they'll stop work for good.'

Mrs Young handed him a cup of coffee. 'Well, that's splendid,' she said. 'From our point of view, I mean.'

Stone regarded her sourly. 'Yes, I thought you'd be pleased. The Professor's fifth column seems to have infiltrated us very successfully.'

'Really?' said the Professor drily. 'You're seriously suggesting, then, that we had something to do with that rockfall?'

'The men have heard about Miss Grant's prediction, and predictions that come true take a good deal of explaining away. But this is what you wanted, isn't it? To hold up the work by fair means or foul?'

Raven moved to stand in front of him. 'As long as they stay down there long enough to get Bill out, we don't care what they do.'

'Well, even that's not certain,' said Stone, 'and if they do pull out and leave Telford to rot, it'll be your fault. The fears they're expressing now are fears that you planted. So you'll have a lot to answer for.'

Raven looked at the Professor in consternation. Could they really be to blame for the present situation? He was sure it hadn't been part of the Professor's plan: how could he possibly have known about Naomi's premonition?

The old man gave him an encouraging nod, reminding him of the reason why the geologist had been summoned to the cabin. He turned back to face him. 'You want Bill out and the strike avoided?'

Stone, sipping his coffee, looked up suspiciously. 'Of course.'

Raven grabbed the file of survey charts and shoved it under his nose. 'Tell 'em to start tunnelling there. In the

Aquarius cave.'

'Why?'

'Because Naomi – Miss Grant – says you'll get through a lot quicker.'

'I see. She's a qualified geologist, is she?'

Castle sniggered. Raven took no notice. 'Listen. When you tried to join Cancer and Capricorn, she predicted danger, right? So she's worth listening to, right? And there aren't any red marks anywhere near, so you can't have tested that rock.'

Stone peered down at the chart. 'Why should that section of rock be any different?'

Naomi spoke with quiet authority. 'Because Aquarius and Cancer are in harmony.'

'But it's further to go. And there's nothing to suggest the going will be any easier.'

'I know,' said Raven, 'but if it works, the strike's off, you've got your tunnel and Bill's safe. If you don't even try, the site's strikebound, you're on the dole and Bill's dead.'

Stone opened his mouth to protest, but found himself speechless. He looked round at the others, lost in unfamiliar seas.

'It'll work,' said Naomi. 'I'm sure of that.'

Stone stared up at her with red-rimmed eyes, then stood up and threw the survey file at Raven. 'All right,' he said angrily. 'What have we got to lose? The new drill-bits should be arriving any moment. I'll switch the crew to the other face.' He stormed out, banging the door behind him.

'Well,' said Castle, perching on the edge of Bill's desk, 'I've got to hand it to you – you've certainly got the power of persuasion. Ever tried selling ice cream to the Eskimos?

You'd make a fortune.'

Raven glanced at Naomi. 'We'd better go down there.'

'Yes.' There was admiration in her eyes.

'And don't forget,' said Castle, 'when they break through, yours is the first face I want to see on that screen.'

'I'll be there,' Raven told him grimly, 'but not because it'll make good television. Because he's my mate.' He grabbed Naomi's arm and pulled her to the door.

Mrs Young called after them. 'Cup of coffee before you go? You ought to have something warm inside you.'

'No time, Mrs Y,' said Raven, pushing Naomi in front of him, 'but thanks anyway.' He disappeared into the evening gloom.

Castle turned to the Professor. 'Remarkable young man,' he said thoughtfully. 'Quite remarkable.'

The Professor smiled. 'Yes, he's doing well, isn't he? Fulfilling all my expectations.'

The clock above the control panel showed that of the original fifteen minutes, only eight were left...

*

The Editor stood with the vicar in the Aquarius cave, watching the construction men fitting a new bit into the heavy drill. 'So they've voted to carry on, eh? To defy the wicked gremlins of the earth?'

The vicar sighed with relief. 'Yes, thank God.'

'So I won't be able to use one of my favourite headlines.'

'What's that?'

'*Strike While the Iron's Hot.*'

'Just as well. I don't suppose Mr Telford's family would think much of it.'

'Perhaps you're right.'

More men appeared, wheeling in the generator. They were followed by the camera crew, who began quickly and efficiently to reassemble their equipment.

'Extraordinary,' said the Editor. 'Rational men behaving like superstitious children. Whatever possessed them?'

'Fear.'

'Fear of what?'

The vicar thought for a moment. 'Of what they don't understand.'

'Of the unknown?'

'Of the uncertain.'

Raven and Naomi appeared at the cave entrance.

'Well, well,' said the Editor drily, 'if it isn't my roving reporter. I hear you've been predicting death and destruction.'

Raven put a protective arm round his companion. 'Don't knock her. She was spot on.'

'Hullo, boss,' said Naomi nervously. 'What are you doing here?'

'Filling in for an errant correspondent, who seems to have forgotten what she's paid for.'

'Give me time. There's a man's life at stake.'

The Editor jerked his thumb at the construction men. 'There's a perfectly capable rescue team taking care of that. Your job was to phone the story through before any other paper got wind of it.'

'Don't worry. It's still an exclusive.'

'No thanks to you,' said the Editor. 'However, now I'm here...' He paused meaningfully.

Naomi looked crestfallen. 'You're taking me off it?'

'This is no place for a professional squabble. I'll leave you something, I promise.'

'The woman's angle, I suppose? "*The Wife and Children who Watch and Wait*"? Thanks a lot.'

Raven poked the Editor in the chest. 'I'll tell you something, Ed. If this story has a happy ending, it'll be down to this ace reporter of yours.'

The silence was suddenly shattered, as the drill, compressor and generator started up again. Naomi dragged Raven out into the Pisces cave, where the noise was a little less deafening. Even so, Raven had to shout to make himself heard.

'I hope Bill wasn't trying to get some kip. That row won't half give him a headache.'

'I'll bet he'd rather hear that than silence.'

'Yeah.' Raven felt the damp rock wall with the palm of his hand. 'Wouldn't fancy being deep inside that lot. At least in solitary, you know you'll get out one day.'

Naomi put a sympathetic hand on his arm, sensing the despair that he was trying so hard to reject. 'Don't worry,' she said softly. 'We'll get him.'

Stone appeared out of the Aquarius cave, sweating profusely. Raven moved up to him. 'Thanks, Mr Stone. You won't regret this.'

'I already am.' The geologist raised his forefinger. 'Just one test-bore, that's all. Three foot maximum – then it's everyone back to the tunnel.'

The cacophony behind him suddenly stopped. Stone turned and dashed back into the cave. Raven and Naomi, the sound of the drill still singing in their ears, looked at each other in dismay.

'Oh no,' whispered Naomi. 'Not again.'

'Maybe it's the equipment they're using.'

They ran through from Pisces to Aquarius, and stared at the rockface in amazement. The solid wall had completely disappeared, and in its place was a gaping black hole. There was no rubble on the floor of the cave – just a thick layer of sand and small pebbles. Max was grinding away with his camera, relaying the phenomenon up to the Portakabin.

Stone was standing with the Editor and the vicar, peering at the hole with total disbelief. 'It's impossible,' he was saying. 'They've only been drilling for a couple of minutes.'

The vicar picked up a handful of sand and let it trickle through his fingers. 'Went through it like putty. There's obviously some sort of fault there.'

Stone caught some of the sand and inspected it closely. 'I don't understand it. I must get this analysed.'

He moved to the cavity and broke off a piece of rock which crumbled at his touch. He stepped back as if he'd been stung by a rattlesnake. 'I just don't understand it,' he repeated.

Raven strode up to him, grabbed his shoulder and spun him round. 'Forget the flaming rock,' he said savagely. 'Get Bill out of there.'

Stone gestured to the construction men. 'On you go, boys.'

The drill juddered into life again, and the onlookers withdrew into the Pisces cave. Raven bellowed up to the camera. 'Prof?'

He was answered by Castle's aristocratic drawl. 'Something we can do for you?'

'Tell the Prof – Naomi seems to have cracked it.'

'In more ways than one, eh? Congratulations.'

'You saw?'

'Everything. The handheld's given us some super close-ups.'

Raven grinned. 'Naomi and me – this week's *Today People*.'

'But definitely. Just be sure you don't miss the climax.'

'Right.' He turned away from the camera and moved back to the others.

The Editor glanced at his watch. 'How long now?'

The vicar shrugged. 'Depends. If we can keep up the same drive-rate, we should reach him soon.'

Raven buried his hands deep in his pockets to stop them shaking. 'Question is – will it be soon enough?'

'I'm sure it will.' The vicar gave him a reassuring pat. 'I don't know how you did it, Raven, but Mr Telford is going to owe you his life. We'd never have got through to him from the tunnel.'

In the next cave, the drill suddenly stopped again. Raven turned and dashed through the entrance, just in time to see the huge drill being withdrawn from the hole.

Stone was shaking his head in amazement. 'If I hadn't seen it, I wouldn't have believed it. There's got to be a sensible explanation.'

'There is.' Raven shouldered him aside and crawled into the hole. 'Bill?' he called. 'It's Raven. You okay?'

No answer. The hole was suddenly flooded with light. Raven turned, to see that Max had trained the handheld camera on him, and one of his colleagues was holding up a portable lamp.

Raven crawled slowly along the narrow passage, his shadow preceding him like a dark, sinister animal. He called again. 'Bill? Can you speak?'

An ominous silence. Ahead of him, the passage veered round to the right, and as he crawled on the light behind him grew dimmer. 'Don't worry, mate,' he shouted into the gloom, 'I'm nearly with you.' The rock ate his voice up like a sponge.

Suddenly, the passage opened out into a large pool of darkness. Raven hesitated: this, surely, must be the cell in which Bill was trapped. But where was he? There was no sign of life, no indication that the trapped man was still there.

Behind him came the sound of grunting and cursing, and Raven realised that Max and the lighting man were following him down the passage. As they drew nearer the darkness ahead began to recede, thrown back by the approaching lamp.

He peered into the shadows, straining his eyes. 'Bill?' he whispered. 'It's me – Raven.'

By now, half the little 'cell' was visible, and only a small area at the rear remained cloaked in impenetrable night. That was where Bill must be lying. He crawled slowly forward again.

Suddenly he stopped, his heart pumping wildly. Out of the inky recess immediately in front of him rose a white object which hung in mid-air, grinning horribly.

It was a human skull…

Chapter Nine

THE DISEMBODIED HEAD REMAINED SUSPENDED in space for what seemed like an eternity. Then it started to glide forwards out of the darkness.

Raven tried to back away, but found he couldn't; his muscles, rigid with shock, refused to obey him.

The skull moved nearer, and as it approached he saw that there was something underneath, supporting it – an arm. At the end of the arm was a shoulder, and above the shoulder, a head. At this point, Max and the lighting man turned the bend in the passage behind him, and the shadowy torso was suddenly exposed to the glare of the lamp. It was Bill.

His face was caked with dirt and grime, but he was grinning from ear to ear as if he and the skull had been sharing the same joke.

'My mate needed rescuing too, Raven,' he croaked hoarsely, 'but I'm afraid you're a bit late for him.'

Raven collapsed to the ground, weak with relief and exhaustion. 'What a nauser. Scaring the pants off me like that – what a right nauser!'

'Sorry, kid.' Bill placed the skull on his chest and patted it fondly. 'Tell you what – I'll make you a present of old Yorick here. As a token of my gratitude and esteem.'

'Thanks a lot.' Raven picked himself up, stuffed the skull into his overalls and started to crawl back down the passage.

'Hold it!' Max was blocking the way, his camera whirring. 'I want a shot of the two of you shaking hands, okay?'

'Oh come on,' said Raven irritably, 'he's been down here long enough.'

But despite his ordeal, Bill seemed in no hurry. 'Listen,' he said cheerfully, 'If the man wants to turn you into a national hero, don't fight it. Let's give him what he wants.'

He held out his hand and Raven took it, feeling like an actor playing a very corny scene.

'Thanks,' said Max. He and the lighting man backed away down the passage. Raven and Bill followed, blinking as they approached the battery of arc-lamps in the Aquarius cave.

Willing hands grabbed them as they emerged into the unaccustomed brilliance, and there was a spontaneous burst of applause from the construction men and the rest of the camera crew. Naomi ran forward to embrace them both, and the Editor and the vicar shook their hands in wordless congratulation. The vicar threw a blanket over Bill's shoulders, and the five of them moved off in the direction of the lift shaft.

They met Castle in the Pisces cave, hurrying towards the scene of the rescue. 'Well done,' he called as he passed, 'you kept us screwed up with tension right to the end – simply screwed up. Don't go wandering off, though. I might need you for some retakes.'

He disappeared into Aquarius, and they heard him congratulating his crew. 'Super, kiddiwinkies – absolutely super. Every frame a poignant masterpiece. What clever little cherubs you all are!'

Bill was staring after him in disbelief. 'Where did he spring from?'

'Don't you recognise him?' asked Naomi. 'That's Clive Castle. You know – *Today People*.'

'Oh.'

Raven was glad to see that Bill was completely unimpressed, but as the lift carried them back to the surface he began to ask himself the same question. Where had Castle sprung from? How did he and his crew happen to be on the spot, so that they could film the rescue? Were they in the vicinity when they heard about the rockfall? If so, who had told them? It was the most incredible coincidence, yet the Professor hadn't seemed at all surprised to learn that the famous television personality had arrived. It was almost as if he had been expecting him.

Outside the Portakabin, the Editor took his leave of them. 'Got to get back to the office,' he said. Then, to Naomi, 'Someone has to file this story.'

She pulled a face. 'Is that a hint? You want me to come with you, right?'

The Editor patted her arm. 'No, you can do the follow-up tomorrow. Stay and minister to Mr Telford. We can build you up as the paper's very own Florence Nightingale.' He moved off in the direction of his car.

Inside the Portakabin, the Professor and Mrs Young were watching Castle interviewing Stone by the hole in the rockface. The Professor switched off the sound as Raven and Naomi helped Bill to a chair.

'How do you feel, Mr Telford? None the worse for wear, I hope?'

'Seems to have escaped with a few scratches,' said the vicar. 'Soon as he's fit, I'll take him to the hospital for a check-up.'

Mrs Young poured a cup of coffee from one of the flasks. 'There we are, Mr Telford,' she said, handing it to him. 'Something to get your circulation going again.'

'Thanks.' Bill sipped the steaming liquid gratefully.

Mrs Young frowned, bent down and peered at his face. 'That's odd.'

'What?'

'You've the same mark as...' She glanced across at Raven, delved into her handbag and produced a mirror, holding it up in front of Bill's face. 'Here – look.'

Bill peered at his reflection – then he, too, looked at Raven. And there was something in his expression that Raven had never seen before. Not in an adult, anyway. There was puzzlement, respect and a touch of fear – the way the lads at Ferndown looked at the Governor when they were being accused of something they didn't do.

Naomi intercepted the glance and moved nearer to inspect the mark on Bill's forehead. 'It's the Pluto symbol,' she said quietly.

'Pluto?' Mrs Young snorted her derision. 'Nonsense,

dear. It's just a bit of dirt.' She produced a handkerchief, wet a corner of it with her tongue and rubbed at the mark. It came off easily.

Raven thought for a moment. If that was the mark he'd had on his forehead after passing out down in the caves, maybe Bill had seen the same vision. But he would have to tread carefully: site managers weren't likely to admit they'd had hallucinations.

'Smell any gas, did you?' he asked casually.

'No.' But from the way Bill avoided his eye, Raven was sure he was lying. He moved round so that he could see the colour of the man's telltale. It was bright red.

'So you were conscious all the time, eh?'

Bill sipped his coffee, his mind far away. For the first time, the strain of the past couple of hours began to show on his face. It was as if he was reliving his period of captivity. It seemed to require a considerable effort to force himself back to the present. 'Conscious? Dunno. May have passed out towards the end. There wasn't much oxygen.'

Raven indicated his telltale. 'Doesn't explain that though, does it?'

'What?' Bill glanced down at his telltale, then up at Raven, mystified. 'No.' Again the look of wonder and curiosity. Raven was dimly aware that their relationship would never be the same again.

The Professor's voice cut like a knife into the silence. 'Can you explain it, Raven?'

Raven turned to face him. 'Me, Prof? No. I don't reckon there is an explanation.'

'There's always an explanation.' Naomi was staring at the Professor with dawning comprehension. 'But not necessarily a practical one.'

The old man smiled at her. 'Very good, my dear.' As if to prevent further speculation, he turned and switched on the sound from below. Castle's voice filled the cabin.

'Mr Stone,' he was saying, 'as the company geologist, can you offer any scientific reason why the rescue team has been able to tunnel through twelve feet of rock in a matter of minutes?'

Stone shook his head. 'No.'

'I understand that the idea of drilling in that particular spot came from a teenage protégé of Professor Young's...?'

'That is correct.'

'... Who knew next to nothing about geology?'

'Also correct.'

'What made you take his advice?'

Stone shrugged. 'It was a last resort. We'd tried everything else.'

'You're telling me that if it hadn't been for this young man, the site manager would still be trapped down here?'

'That's right. It was just a lucky guess, of course...'

Castle turned towards the camera. 'On me, Max.' The camera swung into a large close-up of his face, and he spoke into the lens with hard, dynamic urgency. 'Hullo there,' he said to the millions of viewers who would be watching his programme. 'This week's edition of *Today People* comes to you from deep inside the bowels of the earth. The man you have just been listening to has been part of a grim, tense drama that so nearly ended in tragedy. The fact that tragedy was avoided was due entirely to a young "Person of Today" whom we shall be talking to in a few minutes. But first, the background...'

The Professor shut off the sound and looked at Raven with twinkling eyes. 'Well,' he said, 'you can say what you like about Mr Castle, but he's good at his job. By the time he's finished, you'll be famous.'

And suddenly Raven knew – knew beyond doubt – that it was the Professor who had sent for him. But the certainty raised other doubts. Why had he arranged for Castle to come? Did he know there was going to be an accident? And if so, why had he done nothing to prevent it? There were many secrets behind those shrewd grey eyes, but this was the most impenetrable of all...

*

Later, back at the house, Raven and the Professor sat opposite each other at the kitchen table, while Mrs Young made them cups of cocoa. Raven, his chin cupped in his hands, was staring down at the skull Bill had given him. The eyeless sockets gazed back at him, blank and empty.

'What've you got to grin about, mate?' asked Raven. 'Come on, let us in on it.'

The Professor smiled. 'I should think he's pleased at being released from his solitary confinement. It must have been very lonely down there.'

'Yeah. Wonder who he was.'

'We shall never know that. But we can find out quite a bit about him. Or her.'

'How?'

'There's a friend of mine – forensic pathologist at the hospital – I'll ask him to examine it, if you like.'

Raven picked up the skull and felt the smooth texture of the bone. 'He won't be able to tell much. Not after all this time.'

'Don't you be too sure,' said the Professor. 'He can tell the age, height and build. Approximate date of death. They can make some pretty accurate estimates these days.'

Mrs Young set the cups of cocoa in front of them. 'Well, I think it's gruesome. I don't know what you wanted to bring it back here for.'

Raven held the skull in front of his face and manipulated the jaws like a ventriloquist. 'I needed a home, didn't I?' he intoned in a deep, sepulchral voice, 'a nice warm home after lying about in the cold all them hundreds of years.'

Mrs Young entered into the game. 'Hundreds of years, dear? Are you really that old?'

Raven set the skull back on the table. 'Well, he could be, couldn't he, Prof? You told me that place went back to the Druids.'

'Indeed.'

'Look at him. I know what he's grinning about.'

'What?'

'Me speeding up their tunnel for them. I mean, we got Bill out, but all we've done is saved 'em a bit of time. And we're supposed to be trying to stall 'em, right?'

The Professor sipped his cocoa noisily. 'You did what you had to do, Raven,' he said quietly. And once again, Raven had the uneasy feeling that he was part of some vast, complicated plan…

*

The next day, Naomi picked up Castle at his hotel and drove him back to the construction site. She had been extremely flattered when he had asked her to watch the playback of the rescue film with him, even though it meant getting up an hour earlier so that they could have the Portakabin to themselves.

They sat side by side at the control panel, as the previous night's drama was recreated on the monitor. Naomi was spellbound: now that Bill was safe, she was free to admire the way Max and the camera crew had captured the atmosphere. Despite the immense technical difficulties, it was all there – the frustration and the despair, the excitement and the final joy as Raven and Bill emerged out of the rockface. When the film had been cut and edited, it would make riveting television.

But Castle wasn't satisfied. When the replay came to an end, he remained staring moodily at the blank screen.

'Those chaps weren't nearly dirty enough. We need some close-ups of sweaty faces covered with dirt and grime.'

Naomi was appalled. 'But you can't do that, Clive. You can't play about with the truth. If you cut-in shots taken after the event, you'll be distorting what really happened.'

Castle smiled. 'Not distorting, precious – enhancing. Just gilding the lily a little.'

'The lily doesn't need to be gilded. It's perfect as it is.'

'You think so?'

'Definitely. I mean, the viewers aren't going to be interested in those men as individuals, are they? All you have to show them is the teamwork, the sheer pro-fessionalism. So who wants close-ups? Much more effective if you keep them as shadowy figures, doing their thing.'

Castle thought for a moment. 'Do you know, I believe you're right. Yes. *The Faceless Heroes of the Dark*. I like it.'

He looked at her with new respect. 'Clever you. Pretty too. Has anyone ever told you that?'

Naomi felt herself blushing. 'No one as important as you, kind sir.'

The blue eyes continued to regard her with admiration. 'Seems we're important to each other.'

She wasn't sure how to take this. Could it be that the great man actually fancied her? It was too much to hope for.

'I mean,' Castle went on, 'the programme wouldn't be complete without you.'

'It wouldn't?'

'Absolutely not. I need you on screen. You'll have our male viewers positively palpitating. How about doing an interview for me?'

Naomi looked at her watch. 'Later. I have to get to the office. If I haven't filed my copy by midday, the Editor'll be foaming at the mouth.'

'Okay, you go and file your copy. Maybe I'll call round at your office when I've finished here, and we can do the interview at your desk.'

'If you like. There's an astrological chart on the wall – it'd make a good background.' She stood up and moved to the door.

'Know something?' said Castle. 'I've just made a momentous discovery.'

She turned. 'What?'

'There are actually countryfolk with brains.'

This was a compliment that meant more to Naomi than a hundred flattering remarks about her looks, and all the way back to the office it suffused her in a warm glow. It helped her with her work too: she bashed out her follow-up story with a new confidence, aware that it was one of the best pieces she had ever written.

She zipped the final page out of her typewriter, clipped it with the rest and marched into the Editor's office.

'There you are,' she said, throwing the pages on his desk. 'The inside story. But you won't like it.'

The Editor, who had been staring thoughtfully out of the window, swivelled his chair and frowned. 'Why not?'

'Because it's against editorial policy.'

'Oh?'

'I've suggested the Government is tampering with forces it doesn't understand. That the rockfall was the cave system defending itself against the nuclear invaders.'

The Editor lit his pipe. 'And the Raven-Arthur theory?'

'That's there too.'

He called to the copy-boy. 'Colin?'

The copy-boy appeared at the door, holding a transistor radio to his ear. 'Yes, master?'

'Put that away and take this down to the printing room. Tell 'em it's tomorrow's lead. Front page.'

'Your word is my command, master.' The copy-boy picked up the sheaf of pages and ambled away, whistling tunelessly.

Naomi stared at the Editor, puzzled. 'You haven't even read it.'

'Don't need to. I have every faith.'

'Since when?'

'Since this morning. When the new proprietor called me.'

'New proprietor?'

The Editor puffed contentedly at his pipe. 'There's been

a change of ownership,' he said nonchantly. 'The paper now belongs to an American gentleman who happens to be an environmentalist.'

Naomi collapsed into a chair. 'You're kidding.'

'I never kid – you should know that by now. Our new owner wishes us to remain completely British. He also wishes us to fight against the nuclear reprocessing project with every means at our disposal.'

'It's a miracle.'

'It's the power of the almighty dollar.'

'It's power all right,' said Naomi thoughtfully, 'but it has nothing to do with the dollar.'

It was all beginning to fall into place like pieces of a jigsaw. The different way Bill had looked at Raven after the rescue; Stone bewildered by the ease with which the rock had crumbled; Castle's unexpected appearance in the Gemini cave; the imperturbable calm of the Professor throughout the emergency. And now this fortunate change in the paper's ownership. She thought she knew the answer – but it was a theory so incredible, so way-out, that she needed to have it confirmed. And there was only one person who could do that.

She rushed to the door and blew the Editor a kiss. 'I'm going to talk to Professor Young,' she told him. 'There's more to this story than I realised. And I have a feeling the best is yet to come.' He opened his mouth to protest, but she was gone.

She drove at breakneck speed through the winding country lanes, past fields full of willow-herb and meadowsweet. For the first time, she felt a personal anger against the faceless men in London who had decided that this beautiful countryside should be desecrated to make room for an ugly, dangerous eyesore. They had to be stopped. Which was why the Professor had needed Raven.

She turned in through the gates of his house and screamed to a halt in a shower of flying gravel. Mrs Young was lying full length on the front lawn, staring intently into a bush through a pair of binoculars. Despite the noisiness of the car's arrival, she didn't appear to have heard it.

Naomi got out and walked over to her. 'Morning, Mrs Young...'

'Sh!' The prone figure raised a peremptory hand. 'It's a *Sylvia cucurra* – a lesser whitethroat.'

'Oh.'

Mrs Young's eyes remained glued to the binoculars. 'What do you want, dear?' she croaked in a loud stage-whisper.

'I want a word with the Professor,' said Naomi. 'Is he in?'

'He's in the study. But I don't think you'll get much out of him. He's in one of his grunting moods this morning. Whatever I say, he just goes "Uh".'

Naomi turned and entered the house. The study door was open, and the Professor was writing at his desk, facing away from her. She tapped gently on the door.

'Come in, Miss Grant.' The old man didn't turn, and there was no way he could have known who it was. Perhaps he had seen her from the window. Yet his desk was tucked away in a corner of the room, so he would have needed a periscope. 'Take a seat,' he said, still with his back to her, 'I won't be a minute.'

She flopped down on the sofa, uneasily aware of the

rows of stuffed birds gazing down at her from the walls. She had the strange feeling that the unblinking eyes were scrutinising and assessing her. But it was impossible, of course: she was fantasising like a schoolgirl.

The Professor laid down his pen and turned to face her, smiling. 'Now – what can I do for you?'

But she, too, had a question. 'How did you know it was me, Professor?'

'Ah.' The old man wheeled himself over to the window. 'The trained mind, Miss Grant, is a finely tuned instrument. It sifts a wide variety of apparently insignificant pieces of evidence, and makes sense of them.'

'Evidence? What evidence?'

'I recognised your car.'

So that was it. A simple explanation. Why was it, then, that she found it so difficult to accept?

'Well?' The Professor was looking at her with his head on one side, very like the birds on the shelves around them.

'We've had a bit of luck,' said Naomi quietly. 'The paper's had a change of proprietor and a change of policy. From now on, we're against the nuclear waste project.'

'That is good news.' He didn't sound as surprised as he should have been.

'But not unexpected?'

'I'm a fatalist, my dear. I believe that what will come will come.'

'Is that why you stayed so calm last night? During the rescue?'

The Professor turned and stared out of the window at the cypress trees, swaying gently in the summer breeze. 'No point in – how do they put it these days? – losing one's cool.'

'Especially if you knew they'd get Bill out?'

He glanced at her sharply. 'How could I possibly have known that?'

Naomi rose and wandered round the bookshelves, trailing her fingertips along thick, Moroccan-bound spines. 'I was reading a book the other day,' she said casually, 'a collection of Arthurian legends. There's a theory that the king and his knights didn't die. That they return whenever they're needed.'

She stopped with her back to the old man and waited for his reply. 'Yes,' he said softly.

'Maybe it's more than a theory. I mean, it's a curious coincidence, isn't it? How many people have changed their minds since Raven arrived?'

She turned to face him. The Professor folded his hands across his chest and twinkled at her. 'What about the change in the boy himself? Don't you think that's even more remarkable?'

'Not if you believe in astrology.'

'Astrology?'

'Pluto,' she said, moving to stand in front of his chair. 'The symbol we saw down in the caves. It's supposed to cause radical transformations. To make stable elements unstable…'

'And stable people unstable?'

She held his gaze for a long moment. 'Exactly.'

'You're a very perceptive young lady.'

She waited for him to elaborate, but he seemed to feel that he had said enough. She perched on an arm of the sofa. 'We got a telex from London this morning. The Minister's on his way.'

For the first time, she noticed a crack in the Professor's enigmatic façade. 'But the Appeal's not till the end of the week,' he said, frowning.

'Seems he heard about the rockfall. So he's zooming up here to try and nip any protest in the bud.'

The Professor wheeled himself up to her and snapped at her with fierce intensity. 'We're not ready for him. Not yet.'

He spoke as if he expected Naomi to understand what he was talking about – as if he accepted that she now shared his secret. 'We?' she asked curiously.

'None of us.'

'Not even Raven?'

'He needs more time.'

She decided the time had come to show him that she had guessed. 'Can't the others help?'

The old man stared at her quizzically. 'The others?'

'The rest of his – supporters?'

He nodded, as if giving her permission to pass into his confidence. 'They're not all here yet.'

'You'd better arrange it then, Professor. Fast.'

*

Raven sat with Bill in the Portakabin, waiting for him to speak. The site manager seemed to have suffered no ill effects from his enforced captivity, but Raven sensed there was something on his mind – questions he was dying to ask. While Castle had been with them he had remained at his desk, wrapped in thought. But now that the television inquisitor had disappeared down below to interview some of the construction men, the coast was clear.

'Before the accident,' Bill began awkwardly, 'you heard what I heard down in the caves? Saw what I saw?'

'Yeah.'

'That time you blacked out? Did you see it then?'

'Yeah.'

'And there wasn't any gas – then, or last night. Yet both our telltales registered – something.'

'Yeah.'

Bill contemplated him in silence for a moment. 'What was it, Raven?'

'Dunno, mate.'

'I think you do.'

'Why? Why would I hold out on you?'

'Because you were sent here.'

'Sent?'

'To protect the caves. To make people like me realise we were wrong.'

His subdued, serious manner puzzled Raven. Bill seemed to be looking to him for some sort of lead, to be waiting for orders. But what did he expect him to say? Raven couldn't explain the underground visions either, so there was no point in trying to flannel his way out of it. He decided to try and change the mood.

'You mean I made you see the light?' he said cheerfully. 'That's great. First time in me life I've felt useful.'

'Useful? That's the understatement of the year.' Bill started to pace agitatedly about like a caged lion. 'So how are we going to do it?'

Raven couldn't understand what he was on about. 'Do what?'

'Stop the men from the Ministry. The heathens from

Whitehall.'

So that was it. That's what he was waiting for. He seemed to think that Raven had some magic formula for solving the problem, and all they had to do was put it into practice. Maybe appearances were deceptive. He looked sane enough, but you never could tell. Maybe his experience down in the caves had made him go quietly bananas. Blokes like that had to be humoured.

'How do we stop 'em? Easy. First thing you do is get together with that geologist of yours and say it's not safe down there. Clive Castle'll do the rest.'

Bill shook his head, disappointed. 'That'll just delay the project for a few weeks. We need to make 'em call it off permanently.'

'It'll throw a spanner in the works,' said Raven. 'Give us time to think of something else.'

'But Stone might not agree. He was responsible for the original survey, and if he says it's not safe, he'll be admitting his own incompetence.'

Raven remembered the geologist's face as he examined the crumbled rock. 'Don't worry. He'll agree.'

Bill stared at him. 'How can you be so sure?'

'Because he's confused – not sure of anything any more.'

On cue, the door burst open and Stone rushed in. 'I was right,' he burbled excitedly, 'That stratum is a conglomerate of gravel and shingle, surrounded by a sandy matrix. A sedimentary layer, sandwiched in a metamorphic area of hornblende gneiss.'

Raven grinned and turned to Bill. 'See? He's confused.'

Bill looked irritated. 'Don't show off,' he said, 'What's the verdict?'

'We pull everybody out of there,' said Stone, 'till I've made some more test-bores. It's probably a tilted stratum, so we have to find out where it goes.'

'Pull everybody out, eh? Now?'

'Now.'

Bill hesitated, glanced at Raven as if for confirmation.

Raven barked at him, surprised by the authority in his voice.

'The man said now.'

Bill strode to the talkback and issued the evacuation order through the loudspeaker. Then he wrenched the door open and marched across the site to the lift shaft. Raven and Stone followed, hurrying to keep up with his long strides.

Castle and his crew were already disembarking from the lift. He shrugged apologetically. 'Yes, I know. Women and children first. But I want a shot of the chaps as they come out. Give me the hand-mike, Max.'

When the lift reappeared, carrying the first group of construction men, the crew was ready for them. Max filmed them streaming away from the lift shaft, then pointed the camera at Castle, who spoke fluently into the lens, immediately picking up his commentary.

'... And above ground, the drama continues,' he said. 'Bill Telford, the site manager, who only last night escaped death by a hair's breadth, has just taken a momentous decision. All work on the project is to be stopped, pending a thorough investigation into the cause of the rockfall. Behind me, you can see the men leaving the caves...'

Without warning, he turned, walked over to Raven and pulled him into the shot beside him. 'And here is the young man to whom Telford owes his life. Goes by the unlikely name of Raven. How's it feel to be a hero, eh?'

He shoved the hand-mike under Raven's nose. Raven, taken aback, started to stammer nervously. 'It – it wasn't me. I mean, it was – it was…'

Castle interrupted him impatiently. 'Oh come now. No false modesty. It was you who suggested the successful rescue-plan, wasn't it?'

'I know,' said Raven, still flustered by the unexpectedness of the interview, 'but it was Naomi – Miss Grant – who… who…'

'Cut.' Castle waved to Max and the sound man. 'Hold everything.' The camera stopped whirring. 'Listen, lovey. This is an upbeat show. Do try and give me a bit of viewer-appeal. I mean, this is *Today People*, not *Panorama*. Let's get some *nehnzhhnn!* into it, shall we?'

Raven stared at him. 'Some what?'

Castle put a hand on his shoulder. 'Now look, I've seen a lot of heroics in my time, but what you did to get that poor chappie out was absolutely fantastic.'

Raven looked down at his feet, embarrassed. 'Oh I dunno…'

'I mean it. I have the deepest admiration for you. Now what I want to do is convey that sense of admiration to the people at home, okay? And I can't do that if you just stand there and stutter.'

'I can't help it,' said Raven. 'Anyway, it's not me you want to talk to. It's Naomi. She worked it all out.'

'All right.' Castle punched his arm matily. 'Why don't we give it a rest for the moment. You pop off home, and we'll try again later.'

Raven, grateful for this chance to escape, ran over to the

Portakabin, collected Mrs Young's bike and pedalled off down the road. Just before he turned the corner, he glanced back, to find that Castle and his crew were staring after him. It was extraordinary: they had crowds of other people to interview. What did they want to bother with him for?

The vicar was standing at the entrance of the church as Raven cycled past. He was wearing a cassock, and it was hard to believe this was the same man who had directed the rescue-team so efficiently. The vicar bowed and gave him a mock-salute. Raven waved back, conscious that he was once again the object of an adult's respectful attention. What the hell was the matter with them all?

He freewheeled up the drive of the Youngs' house and leant his bike against the wall just outside the front door. He saw Mrs Young lying on the lawn, but decided not to disturb her. She was probably on the trail of a great-crested peewit or something.

It was only then that he noticed Naomi's car. What was she doing here? She'd told him that she would be up to her eyes at the office all day.

He let himself into the house, and heard voices coming from the study. Naomi and the Professor. He stopped outside the door, listening.

'How did you know, Professor?' Naomi was saying.

'Know?'

'About Raven.'

'What about him?'

'That he was – special. He's the Arthur, isn't he? The new one...'

Raven remained rooted to the spot, unable to believe his ears.

Chapter Ten

HE PUSHED THE DOOR OPEN and grinned at them. 'Arthur? Me? Leave off, Scoop. A bloke with my record couldn't be an MP, let alone a king.'

Amazingly, the Professor seemed to be treating the proposition seriously. 'What you were doesn't matter any more, Raven,' he said softly, 'It's what you *are* that matters. A true leader has no need of the trappings of power. All he needs is a natural authority.'

'And you reckon that's what I've got, eh? – a natural authority?' He moved to sit on the sofa next to Naomi. 'Tell that to the screws at Ferndown, Prof – they're the ones who give the orders.'

'Till now.' The wise grey eyes were boring into him like lasers.

Raven shifted uncomfortably. 'Yeah, well… do me a favour, will you? Don't take the mickey – I'm not in the mood.'

But the old man pressed him inexorably. 'Some are born great. Some achieve greatness. Some have greatness thrust upon them!'

'And some thrust it right back again an' all.' Raven suddenly noticed the stuffed merlin standing on the Professor's desk. 'Here – what's my bird doing over there?'

'I was showing it to Miss Grant.'

'Why?'

'I thought it might interest her.'

Raven turned to Naomi, whose eyes had never left his face since he entered the room. It was great to be the object of her attention, but he was gloomily conscious that it wasn't because she fancied him. She was looking at him as if there were a glass case round him, as if he were something in a museum.

'Since when did you get interested in birds?' he asked her.

'Since I saw that one!' Then, lowering her voice to a whisper, 'What is it, Raven?'

'It's a...' He stopped abruptly, realising that his answer would only confirm her absurd theory.

'Yes?'

'A merlin,' he said gruffly.

She glanced at the Professor. 'Fascinating. Well, I must get back to the office. Clive Castle's coming to interview me.'

Raven was irritated by the way she patted a stray hair into place. So she still hadn't got Castle out of her system. 'I'm coming too,' he said.

*

Meanwhile, a long black limousine was gliding noiselessly up to the construction site. A chauffeur got out and opened the back door for his passenger – a fat, self-important little man wearing a dark coat and carrying an umbrella.

The passenger stared across at the television van with *MTV* printed on it, and thoughtfully smelt the carnation in his buttonhole. 'Wait here, Charles,' he said to the chauffeur, and marched across to the Portakabin.

Inside, Castle was interviewing Bill Telford. He looked round irritably as the new arrival entered.

'Cut,' he said to the crew. Then, turning to the visitor, 'Minister, I'm trying to do an interview.'

The minister smiled frostily. 'So I see. Well, you can interview me first, Castle. I haven't got much time.'

Castle sighed. 'I've done countless interviews with you. And my audience is getting just the teensiest bit tired of the same old faces week after week.'

'If people want open government, that's the price they have to pay. Come on – let's get it over with. You can call the programme *Power to the People*. Play on words, d'you see? There's the nuclear power aspect as well as the…'

'No,' said Castle firmly.

'What d'you mean – no?'

'I don't want you on the programme.'

The minister stared at him incredulously. 'Don't want me?'

'Talking heads are boring – especially yours. Last time you appeared on the show, the ratings dropped through the floor.'

Max sniggered. The minister ignored him. 'Ratings? Is that all you care about?'

'Frankly – yes.'

'Suppose I were to put in an official complaint to MTV? About the one-sided picture you're presenting?'

Castle took him by the arm and led him to the door. 'Waste of time, old sprout – I'm much too popular. You're staying at the King's Arms?'

'Yes.'

'See you for drinkies tonight, then. Bye-bye.'

He shoved him unceremoniously outside, and closed the door. 'All right, Max. On we go.'

Max nodded to the sound man and trained the camera on Bill, sitting at his desk in front of the model of the cave system. Castle sat on the other side of the desk with his back to the camera. 'Now then, Mr Telford. Could you show me exactly where the accident occurred?'

Bill picked up a pencil and indicated the place on the model. 'Here. We were tunnelling through solid granite. There was no reason for it to collapse.'

'No geological reason?'

'That's right.'

'What about the seam the boy found? The layer of shale, or whatever it was. Could you point it out for me?'

Bill indicated the Aquarius cave with his pencil. 'It started here. Though where it goes is anyone's guess.'

'So it could extend further than you thought? Across the roof of the tunnel, perhaps? Maybe that's what caused it to collapse.'

'It's possible,' said Bill wearily, throwing down the pencil. 'Anything's possible.'

The door burst open again and the minister reappeared, followed by Stone. He stood in front of Bill's desk, looking like an angry goldfish.

'Telford,' he said grimly, 'will you please explain why you have ordered your men to evacuate the caves?'

Max lowered his camera, but Castle signalled to him to keep it running. The sound man got the message and inched the microphone nearer to the minister, who was too furious to notice.

Bill shrugged. 'Should have thought it was obvious.'

'One isolated fall? That's no reason to stop work.'

'I'm not risking the lives of my men till we've made some more tests.'

'The original survey was extremely thorough,' said the minister, glancing at Stone. 'There's absolutely no need for this… this scaremongering.'

It was Bill's turn to become angry. 'You wouldn't say that if you'd been trapped down there.'

The minister put both hands on his umbrella and leant across it, speaking slowly and deliberately, as if he were making a speech in the House of Commons. 'You realise that if this gets out, there'll be a national outcry? And the whole project might have to be abandoned?'

'Are you prepared to take the responsibility, minister?' Stone intervened, 'because we're not.'

The minister rounded on him, red in the face. 'Lot of old women, that's what you are. It's the old story – give the British workman the slightest excuse to down tools and he's off to the nearest pub.'

'Why don't you join them?' said Bill sourly. 'You might learn something.'

'Don't be impertinent. There's a great deal of public money invested in this project. So if you can't get your men back to work, I'll find someone who can.' He flounced out of the cabin, slamming the door behind him.

'And to think people actually voted for him,' said Bill.

Castle pointed to the spools of the sound man's tape recorder, which were still running. 'Don't worry, dear heart,' he grinned. 'That little outburst has been recorded for posterity. And I'll see to it that it costs him his job.'

Bill shook his hand in silent congratulation.

*

When Castle arrived at the *Herald* office, he had the tape recorder with him. Raven, Naomi and the Editor crowded round the machine as he rewound the spools. 'Listen to this,' he said, 'It's dynamite.'

They listened to the minister sounding off about the laziness of the British workman with incredulous delight. 'It's great,' said the Editor, puffing contentedly at his pipe. 'We'll print it word for word – without comment. It'll do far more damage than an editorial.'

Castle held up a long, well-manicured forefinger. 'One condition.'

'Yes?'

'You mention yours truly. And the forthcoming pro-gramme. A hint of scandal does wonders for the viewing figures.'

'Of course. You scratch my back and I'll scratch yours.'

Castle grinned. 'No offence, but – leave that to Miss Grant, would you?'

Raven waited for the Editor to make some comeback, but he was looking fondly at Naomi as if he soon expected to lose her. 'Look after her, Mr Castle,' he said, patting her on the cheek. 'She's a very special correspondent.'

'I know.' Castle took one of the spools off the machine and handed it to him. 'Why don't you get your secretary to make a transcript of this?'

'Right.' The Editor disappeared into his office.

Raven glanced from Castle to Naomi, feeling more and more out of his depth. Things were happening between them, and he was at a loss to know what to do about it. That they fancied each other had been obvious since their first meeting, but there was now an unspoken intimacy about their relationship that was very disturbing. How could it have developed so fast? He'd had two weeks' start, yet his rival had managed to overtake him in less than twenty-four hours. He must try to make up for lost time, to remind Naomi that he was still around.

'Special correspondent, eh?' he said, trying to sound offhand. 'You're special to me an' all, Scoop. And I found you first, don't forget.'

Her expression was tender, understanding – but distant. As if she were talking to her favourite aunt. 'Sorry, Raven. You're too late.'

He stared at her, his stomach churning. 'Too late?'

'You should've told me I had brains.'

'What d'you need telling for?'

'A woman always needs telling. That's something you'll learn when you're a bit older.'

So there it was – the final brush-off. The hopelessness of the situation numbed him: she couldn't have hurt him more if she had smacked him in the face. He swallowed, tried to think of something flip to say, but for the first time in his life he was at a loss for words. She was out of his reach, and nothing would bring her back again: all through their lives, the devastating age-gap would remain, and the three or four years that separated them could never be bridged.

Castle seemed oblivious of the torture he was suffering. 'I was wondering,' he said to Naomi, perching on the edge of her desk, 'how would you feel about coming to work for MTV?'

Her eyes grew round with excitement. 'You mean it?'

The immaculate white teeth gleamed at her. 'I don't say anything I don't mean, precious – except on the programme, of course. You'll have to start as a researcher, but if you turn out to be as photogenic as you look I might let you handle some of the interviews.'

'Me? Oh Clive...'

Her gushing adoration was too much for Raven. He turned away in disgust.

'It'll be a hard grind, of course,' Castle went on. 'You'll have to be at my beck and call morning, noon and night.'

Raven headed unnoticed for the door. Behind him, he heard Naomi continue to gush. 'I don't mind. I've always wanted to get into television.'

'And I warn you – I'm a terrible slave-driver.'

'I'm used to slave-drivers. I've worked with one for three years.'

Raven opened the door and turned gloomily to Naomi. 'Going to drop me, are you?' he asked. But the moment the words were out of his mouth he regretted them: the double meaning took him by surprise.

She was too wrapped up in Castle to notice. 'Sorry, Raven. I've got to hang on here. Clive's going to do an interview with me as soon as the crew arrive.'

'Why don't you hang on too?' said Castle. 'We still have our little retake to do, don't forget.'

'Later.' Raven closed the door softly behind him. He was alone again. Well, he was used to that. If she preferred berks like Castle, there was nothing he could do about it – except show her he could survive without her. The solitary survivor, that was him. He didn't need anyone: never had, and never would. He'd make it on his own.

*

The Professor and the vicar were sitting out in the garden, sipping glasses of sherry. Forty years separated them, yet their minds were so attuned that they might have been brothers. The afternoon sun bathed the two men in a mellow glow, and it was hard to believe that on such a perfect summer day there was a crisis to be faced.

The vicar sighed. So far, he hadn't mentioned the reason for his visit, but it couldn't be delayed any longer. Time was getting short.

'The Minister's arrived,' he said, watching a squirrel run up the trunk of one of the elms.

'I know,' said the Professor. 'Bill Telford called me.'

'Anything I can do?'

'I'll let you know.'

A bee droned lazily past them and settled on one of the roses.

'Is everyone here?' asked the vicar.

'Tonight. They'll all be here tonight.'

'You've something up your sleeve?'

The Professor shrugged. 'It's not up to me.'

167

The vicar glanced at him, troubled. 'The boy? Is he ready?'

'I don't know. That's what worries me.'

So even the old man wasn't sure. They must face the crisis with an unknown quantity as their spearhead – march into battle with nothing but hope and prayer to depend on. Still, one mustn't underestimate the power of a prayer.

The vicar drained his glass and stood up. 'See you tonight, then.'

The Professor nodded. 'Push me inside before you go, there's a good fellow. I've had enough sun for today.'

The vicar wheeled him up the steps into the hall and took his leave. The Professor watched him stride away into the heat-haze at the end of the drive, then turned and propelled himself slowly to the study door.

His wife was sitting at his desk, reading the half-written document he had carelessly left on the blotter. She looked round guiltily as he appeared in the doorway, and they stared at each other in embarrassment.

'Not like you to pry, my dear,' said the Professor gently.

'I was looking for some labels. I couldn't help seeing it.'

'No, I suppose not. It was my fault.' He wheeled himself over to her, took the document from her and shut it away in a drawer.

Her hands suddenly had nothing to do, and they twisted nervously in her lap. 'Why are you making your will, dear?'

He smiled reassuringly at her. 'Because I'm getting on. And it's time I put my affairs in order.'

'Don't be silly, James. You're just run down – depressed at the thought of losing the Appeal. What you need is a tonic.'

He took one of her twisting hands and held it tightly. 'What I need is your assurance that you won't grieve for me. I shan't be far away.'

She jerked her hand away and frowned at him. 'I don't know what you're talking about,' she said crossly. 'And you're starting to make me depressed. After spotting that splendid lesser whitethroat too – it's really very thoughtless of you.'

'I'm sorry.' If only he could tell her everything, teach her to accept her destiny as he had learned to accept his. But it would be no good – she wouldn't know what he was talking about. Close as they were, there was a part of his life she could never share.

'Promise me one thing, my dear,' he said, wheeling himself over to the merlin.

'What?'

He removed the glass case and let his hand rest gently on the bird's head. 'After I'm gone – burn this.'

She stared at him in astonishment. 'Burn it?'

'He's like the phoenix. The survival of his species depends on it.'

'Rubbish.' She stood up and bustled to the door. 'There are plenty of merlins about – if you know where to look. I should stick to archaeology, if I were you.'

She disappeared into the hall, just as Raven entered through the front door. Noticing his grim expression, she stopped. 'My, my. We do look pleased with life. What's happened to Mr Smile today?'

Raven scowled at her, and she scuttled off in the direction of the kitchen. He moved to the bottom of the stairs and had just begun to climb when the Professor called to him from the study.

He pulled a face. The last thing he wanted was to talk to anyone, but he couldn't just ignore the old man. Not after all he'd done for him.

He turned back and went into the study. 'Yeah? What d'you want, Prof?'

The Professor's hand was still resting on the merlin's head. The two pairs of eyes were staring at him unnervingly, and Raven looked down at his feet to avoid them.

'What's the matter?' asked the Professor quietly.

'Just fed up.'

'She's not for you, you know. I tried to warn you.'

So he knew. It was incredible how sharp the Professor was, how he always seemed to be one step ahead of you.

Raven flopped wearily down in a chair. 'She's going away with... with...'

'Yes. I know.'

'She said it'd've been all right if I'd told her she had brains.'

'That's just an excuse. It would never have been – all right.'

'Why not?'

The Professor's expression softened with sympathy and understanding. 'You were born a few years too late, Raven. I'm afraid you were destined for sadness.'

Raven frowned, puzzled. 'What d'you mean?'

'It's in your stars. If Naomi had read your horoscope, she could probably have told you.'

'Yeah?'

'However...' The old man paused, surveying him with a touch of anxiety, 'you're also destined for very important work. And you were born at exactly the right time for that.'

'What work?'

The Professor delved into his breast pocket and produced a sheet of paper. 'I've had the forensic report on that skull. It belonged to a sixteen-year-old male, about five feet ten inches tall. How tall are you, Raven?'

'Five-ten.' Raven felt a sudden irritation. 'Forget it, Prof. Don't start all that Arthur stuff again. Makes me feel like some sort of freak.'

'I'm trying to tell you that you're indispensable,' said the Professor. 'We can't do without you.'

Raven stood up. 'Well, you're going to have to.'

'What do you mean?'

'I can't take any more. I'm going back to Ferndown.'

'No!' There was alarm in the old man's voice. 'You can't!'

'Why not? I've got to go back soon anyway. It may not be as cushy as this number, but at least I can understand what people are on about.'

The Professor wheeled himself forward and looked up at him with blazing eyes. 'You must stay till the Appeal. You must!'

Raven smiled. 'Careful. You're beginning to sound like a screw.'

'Raven, please. There's a meeting tonight. I want you to come with me.'

'Meeting?'

'I can't explain now. Trust me – everything will suddenly become clear to you, I promise…'

*

That evening, at dusk, Mrs Young drove them to the construction site. Raven was intensely curious: the Professor's guarded hints had whetted his appetite for this strange meeting, and he couldn't wait to find out who would be present. Nor could he imagine why they wanted him to be there: he supposed it was something to do with this very important work for which the old man had told him he was destined, but why did they need him? No one had ever needed him before.

The Professor had refused to answer any more questions, telling him mysteriously that the time for understanding was near. If he would just be patient for a little while longer, all would be revealed to him. But for the first time, Raven sensed a doubt behind the grey eyes that was very disturbing. It was as if a rock on which he had been leaning suddenly began to disintegrate, leaving nothing between him and the ground but air.

They sat in silence as the car careered between tall hedgerows through the gathering gloom. Every now and then the headlights would pick out a rabbit lolloping across the road in front of them and there would be a sudden jerk as Mrs Young jammed on the brakes. Raven reckoned she must have worn about half an inch off the disc-pads during the short journey, but the Professor endured the bone-shattering ride without complaint. He stared out of the window at the passing countryside, tense and preoccupied.

They turned into the construction site and parked near the Portakabin. Light was streaming from the cabin windows, and Raven assumed that this was where the meeting was to take place. But he was wrong. As soon as Mrs Young had driven away, the Professor pointed to the group of rocks.

'Up there,' he said.

Raven wheeled him up the narrow path to the rocks, their shadows preceding them like advance scouts. It was a steep little climb, and by the time they reached the top of the incline he was panting for breath. Just outside the rock circle he stopped and looked round. The place seemed silent and deserted.

'Hurry up,' said the Professor crossly. 'They're waiting.'

'Where?'

'Use your eyes, boy. There – by the rocks.'

And suddenly, Raven saw. In front of each of the smaller rocks, half hidden by their shadows, someone was standing. Only the twelfth rock – the largest of all – was unoccupied.

Raven walked slowly into the circle and blinked with astonishment. Five of the faces were new to him, but the others he knew well – they were all mates of his. There was Bill… the Editor… the vicar… Stone… Castle… and Naomi. His heart jumped as he saw her: was it only this afternoon that they had all listened to Castle's tape in the *Herald* office? It seemed like an eternity ago.

But why didn't any of them say anything? Why were they just standing still like that? He began to feel uneasy: were they a coven of witches or something, intending to sacrifice him to the moon? It just wasn't natural, the way they were staring at him in calm silence, like an audience in a theatre just after the curtain has gone up, waiting for the play to begin. They might at least say hello.

He was just beginning to wish he had stayed at home, when he heard the squeak of the Professor's chair behind him. He turned, trying to hide his nervousness.

'This the meeting then, Prof?'

'This is the meeting. The coming together…'

It didn't sound too good. The chaplain at Ferndown talked like that about the Sunday service. Maybe there was to be some sort of religious ceremony to celebrate mid-summer or something. He just wished they'd get on with it.

He glanced warily round at the ring of impassive faces standing under the carved rock-symbols, then back at the Professor. 'Well? Aren't you going to say something?'

'No.'

'Why not? Looks like they're waiting for you.'

'Not me, Raven…'

He paused expectantly, and suddenly Raven heard, far below him in the caves, the eery, magical sounds that had accompanied his subterranean vision. The jangling of a harness, the stamp of hooves, voices murmuring low and occasional bursts of laughter.

Then, as he watched, something at the edge of the circle began to glow in the darkness. On the large empty rock, beneath the symbol of the Centaur, appeared another symbol which seemed to hover in mid-air, luminous and transparent. It was the Pluto sign.

The hair at the base of his neck bristled, and he pointed fearfully. 'Prof! Look!'

The old man sounded completely unruffled. 'It's your appointed place, Raven.'

Raven stared at him for a long moment, suddenly aware that he was in the presence of a power that made nuclear energy seem primitive by comparison. He felt like a puppet, in the hands of a benevolent puppet-master. And dimly, he began to realise what he had been created for.

'Go,' said the Professor softly, pointing to the large Centaur-rock. He wheeled himself away into the darkness, leaving Raven alone – an actor at the mercy of his audience.

But Raven was no longer afraid. He was not sure yet what was expected of him, but with the newfound confidence the Professor had given him he knew he could fulfil any expectation. He looked round at the circle of eyes fixed unwaveringly on his face, and strode over to the empty rock. As he did so, the Pluto sign slowly dissolved until it vanished completely.

In the shadow of the rock, he turned and confronted his eleven companions. They were still standing in quiet anticipation, waiting. But for what? Unless someone told him what to say, they could be there all night…

Chapter Eleven

He looked at Naomi, standing under the Libra symbol, her face pale in the light spilling up from the Portakabin windows. She was smiling slightly, as if she knew that Raven would find the right words no matter how long it took. Raven wished he shared her confidence; he hadn't felt so tongue-tied since the Governor caught him making grappling-hooks in the metal shop.

He couldn't see the Professor, but he knew he was still there, sitting in the darkness outside the circle like a falcon guarding its nest. A merlin watching its young learn how to fly.

Then, wafting through the night, came the old man's voice, soft and low. 'Speak!' And suddenly, without effort, the words came...

'We must fight!' Raven heard himself saying. 'Now as always. Today as yesterday. We must defend what is ours.'

His voice echoed away across the lonely moorland, and

the only sound was the wind whistling gently through the stones. His followers were listening to him with rapt attention, and he knew instinctively that they would do whatever he told them without question. The power that he had sensed in the Professor was now flowing through him like an electric current, and he realised now why the old man had needed him. He alone could do what had to be done.

He shivered. The electric current had nothing to do with warmth, and the wind was giving him goose-pimples. There was no point in catching pneumonia. 'How about going inside?' he said. 'I'm freezing to death out here.'

He marched out of the circle and down the path to the Portakabin, followed by the others. There was no sign of the Professor, but Raven no longer needed him. The puppet now had a mind and will of his own.

They crowded into the cabin and ranged themselves round the walls. Castle picked up his tape recorder and looked questioningly at Raven. 'The interview? Now?'

Raven nodded and perched on the edge of Bill's desk while Castle positioned the microphone. Then he switched on the machine and began.

'So we must fight to defend what is ours. Does that mean violence?'

This time, there was no stuttering or stammering. Raven replied easily and fluently. 'The violence has already started,' he began. 'They're destroying the countryside to make way for a lot of industrial garbage. They're starting a dangerous game with no idea of how it's going to finish. And they're dumping a lot of poisonous waste which might top us all one day. What's more violent than mass murder?'

Castle smiled his approval. 'So you see yourself as the

guardian of the future?' he went on. 'As a representative of the younger generation battling against the short-sightedness of your elders?'

'Listen,' said Raven sternly, 'we're responsible for the kids that aren't even born yet. You reckon they'll thank us for burying stuff that'll still be deadly in a hundred years' time? Or a thousand? Maybe even a million? If this was a problem we couldn't solve, there'd be some excuse. But we can solve it – just by saying no.'

There was a spontaneous burst of applause, and Castle switched off the machine. 'Fantastic,' he said, looking at Raven with respect and admiration. 'We'll superimpose that over some shots of the construction site, the open countryside and the model of the reprocessing plant. It'll have impact with a capital I.'

Raven looked doubtful. 'Maybe.'

'What's the matter? Don't you like it?'

'Some stupid kid sounding off about a subject he doesn't understand. That's what they'll say.'

'It'll make 'em stop and think.'

'But it won't change their minds. We need something stronger. Much stronger…'

Naomi frowned. 'Such as?'

'Dunno. Let's see what we've got. Bill?'

'I've called a halt pending Stone's investigation,' said Bill. 'That should carry some weight.'

Raven turned to the geologist. 'Stone?'

'There's that seam of shale. We don't know where it goes. Could delay the project for months.'

'Vicar?'

'It's all in my interview with Clive,' said the vicar. 'The

unexpectedness of the rockfall. The hazards of the rescue operation. The fact that Bill's lucky to be alive. Et cetera, et cetera.'

Raven glanced at the Editor, who shrugged. 'Our new proprietor has ordered a change of policy. We're mounting a big campaign against the project. Our line will be that it's both a stain on the countryside and a potential killer.'

'Naomi?'

'I'm concentrating on the Minister. Doing a biography called *Local Boy Makes Bad*. There's plenty of material, believe me. Political backstabbing, errors of judgement, speeches full of meaningless platitudes.'

'Clive?'

Castle hesitated. 'There's my programme,' he said thoughtfully, 'but frankly, it worries me.'

'Why?'

'Because it's turning into a propaganda exercise. We'll be accused of bias – rightly – and we'll get a lot of stick from the trial-by-television lobby.'

'We won't get anywhere with the soft sell,' said Naomi.

'We won't get anywhere with oversell either. What we're presenting is an ecological commercial. We're not even attempting to present the opposite point of view.'

'Why should we?' asked Bill. 'That's the Minister's job.'

'Right,' said Raven. 'That programme they did, putting the official line – the Prof showed it me when I first arrived – that was tough, hard-hitting. Can't we do the same?'

'Not without jeopardising our case,' said Castle.

There was a sudden, uncomfortable silence. Gloom hung like a pall in the air.

Then Naomi brightened. 'What if we concentrate on the

practical side of it? The suitability of the caves as a dumping ground? Use the rockfall, possible gas-pockets – that sort of thing.'

'We'd have to come up with something really concrete,' said Castle, 'and Stone's got nothing to offer.'

'No, 'fraid I can't help,' said Stone, 'Not yet anyway. The powers-that-be are saying the fall was my fault for not anticipating the shale-stratum. And as for gas – there's no cause for concern there.'

Raven looked round at the depressed expressions on the faces of his troops and made a conscious effort to rally them.

'Look. We may be in bad shape at the moment, but there's still a couple of days before the Hearing. Maybe if we blind 'em with science – hammer 'em with ecology, technology and any other *-ology* we can come up with – maybe it'll all add up to something pretty convincing.'

'Maybe,' said Naomi, looking far from convinced.

He put a comforting hand on her shoulder. 'Cheer up, Scoop. We managed to convert Bill, Stone and your Editor. That's a three-goal lead before we kick off. And there's no knowing how many we'll score once the game starts.'

There were tears in her eyes, but now there was hope behind them. She looked up at him in complete trust, and he realised with a pang how much she and the others depended on him. Without him, they were lost. Whatever happened, he mustn't let them down. He must think of something.

*

But the day of the Hearing arrived, and his mind was still a blank. Naomi had offered him a lift to the town hall and the Professor had urged him to accept, saying that he and Mrs Young wanted a little time to themselves before the battle began.

So she called at the house shortly after eight-thirty, and they drove into town through the early morning haze. She had put the roof down – it was going to be another glorious day – and Raven sprawled in the passenger seat, watching her hair flying in the wind. She really was the most fantastic girl. If only… But there was no point in thinking about what might have been. Despite the fact that they sat side by side, she might as well have been in another universe. So near and yet so far.

No, the past was dead. Only the present and the future were still alive, and he must concentrate on them. He must keep all his senses alert, so that if a possible solution presented itself he wouldn't miss it. He knew that the answer couldn't be far away, but it remained tucked away in the corner of his brain, tantalisingly out of reach.

As they drew up outside the town hall, Raven saw Castle and his camera crew stationed at the top of the steps. He was interviewing each new arrival in search of usable material: if they could get the enemy to damn themselves out of their own lips as the Minister had done it was worth a hundred impassioned speeches by their own supporters. But there wasn't much chance of that – they'd all be very much on their guard.

Raven grabbed Naomi's arm and hurried her up the steps. Castle gave them a cheerful grin, which suddenly changed to a grim scowl as he saw another car draw up below. The three of them watched as the chauffeur opened the back door and the Minister climbed out, smiled towards a group of photographers clustered on the pavement and started to run up the steps two at a time.

The unaccustomed exercise was too much for him, and he had to stop half-way and catch his breath before continuing to the top at a more sedate pace. He held out his hand to Castle, panting with exertion.

'Morning, Castle. Glad you're going to make a record of these proceedings. People can't say we didn't have a full and frank discussion, what? Justice seen to be done, and all that?'

Castle ignored him. He moved away to greet two of the strangers who had been present at the meeting among the rocks, and the Minister was left with egg on his face, looking furious. Raven noted with satisfaction that Max had recorded his expression for posterity.

He and Naomi turned and went inside, following a stream of people down a long corridor and into a large council-chamber. Rows of chairs had been set out in the body of the hall, at least half of which were already occupied. On a dais at the far end of the room was a long trestle table, behind which sat several important-looking men whispering earnestly to each other.

One man sat alone, arms folded, staring down at the rows of chairs with a bored, disdainful air – as if he'd had to endure this sort of thing many times before, and resented being taken away from more essential work. He was tall, with sleek grey hair and a well-groomed moustache. Raven had never seen anyone who looked more distinguished.

'Who's that?' he asked Naomi as they took their seats at the rear of the room.

She followed his gaze and frowned. 'Sir Lewis Gurney – a real nuclear diehard. And the two men next to him are his assistants at the Department of Industry.'

'The heavy mob,' muttered Raven sourly.

'Right. They'll be impressive witnesses, those three. We've no one to match them.'

'If only we could've converted one of them.'

Naomi pulled a face. 'You'd have as much chance of converting the Minister.'

The popping of flash-bulbs behind them made them turn. The Minister was standing in the doorway, surrounded by reporters and photographers. Now that he was once again the centre of attention he had regained his good humour, and was smiling and waving at Sir Lewis and his colleagues up on the platform.

'Now then,' he said, projecting his voice so that it boomed through the hall, 'where's the young chap we have to thank for the rescue?'

One of the reporters pointed to Raven, and the Minister marched over to him with his retinue of pressmen, like a whale surrounded by pilot-fish.

'Raven?' Raven stood up. 'I understand you made a lucky guess the other night. Stuck a pin in the plan and came up with a rotten seam or something?'

Raven shifted uncomfortably from one leg to the other. 'There was more to it than that.'

'You mean it wasn't just a pin? What else did you use – a water-divining rod?' The pressmen laughed. 'Anyway, we got the poor fellow out, that's the main thing. But I hear you're against the project, is that true?'

'Yeah.'

The Minister smiled unpleasantly. 'Well, you're going to lose this Appeal, so you're not going to have much luck today. But I can offer you my congratulations and wish you the best of luck for the future.'

He grabbed Raven's hand, put a patronising arm round his shoulder and turned, posing blatantly for a photograph. Another bulb flashed. Raven blinked, and by the time his eyes had refocused the Minister was already half-way to the platform.

Naomi stood up angrily. 'The man's incorrigible. He'll do anything for publicity. Henry!' The photographer who had taken the picture turned guiltily. 'I want that negative.'

She held out her hand, and the photographer sheepishly took out the roll of film and gave it to her. 'I know,' he said, 'I was set up.' He drifted away with the rest of the pressmen.

The Minister stood behind the trestle table and banged a gavel till the audience's chatter subsided. 'I declare this meeting open,' he said, 'and I call upon Sir Lewis Gurney to sum up the Government's case for the benefit of those who were not present at the earlier Inquiry.'

As Sir Lewis stood up, Raven looked round anxiously. 'Where's the Prof?' he whispered to Naomi. 'He should be here by now.'

She squeezed his arm. 'Don't worry, there's plenty of time. Sir Lewis'll drone on for hours.'

'This is a region,' Sir Lewis began, 'which was designated long ago as a development area – a place to which new industry should be directed. Unemployment, particularly among the young, among school leavers, has for many years remained at an unacceptable level…'

A murmur of approval ran through the audience. Raven

frowned. 'He sounds so flaming reasonable,' he growled. 'By the time he's finished, he'll have everyone eating out of his hand.'

'We haven't had our say yet,' Naomi whispered back, 'Wait till the Prof gets going – he's pretty impressive too. And a lot less boring.'

'So much for the social background,' Sir Lewis went on. 'And now the practical reasons for selecting the cave complex as a storage depot for nuclear waste. Certain fears have been expressed – understandable fears – but believe me, they are groundless. Once sealed underground the toxic material will be entirely safe. We have recently developed a process for turning liquid nuclear waste into a form of glass, and each cylinder will be welded into place with molten rock…'

Naomi nudged Raven and indicated the door. Mrs Young was wheeling the Professor into the room. The old man sat huddled in his chair, looking pale and drawn, but Raven was too relieved to notice his appearance. He was there – that was the important thing – in time to lead the counter-attack.

Sir Lewis fixed his audience with a stern glare, like a father lecturing his wayward children. 'I repeat – this site satisfies every one of our safety requirements. No earth tremor has ever been recorded in this part of the country. There is no circulating groundwater which, in the event of a leakage, could spread radioactivity, and there will be no necessity for the plutonium waste to travel outside the processing area. It will be dumped straight from the plant into the cave system below…'

Raven fidgeted in his chair. He felt so helpless, listening

passively as the quiet, articulate man justified the unjustifiable. He must get away and think; perhaps some last-minute masterstroke would occur to him.

He hissed in Naomi's ear. 'Let's go.'

She stared at him in astonishment. 'Go? Where?'

'Anywhere. I've got to get out of here.'

They stood up and made their way along the row to the aisle. Raven waved to the Professor, who nodded, as if he knew where they were going even if they didn't.

Sir Lewis's voice pursued them out of the door. '… So the site bristles with advantages. No earth movement, safety from accidental leakage, a burial ground beyond the reach of possible terrorist attacks. We offer employment without risk, a huge capital investment in this community without danger. If I may borrow a phrase from President Franklin D. Roosevelt, you have nothing to fear but fear itself…'

Raven hurried Naomi out of the building, down the steps and into her car. 'You sure you know what you're doing?' she asked, starting the engine.

'No.'

'Seems to me we shouldn't be going away from the action.'

Raven rested his arm along the back of her seat. So near and yet so far. 'That's not action,' he said scornfully. 'That's just talk.'

'So where is the action?'

He thought for a moment. 'The site. It's got to be at the site.'

'Why?'

'The cave system's proved it's capable of defending itself. All it needs is a little help.'

'What sort of help?'

'Dunno. Maybe we'll know when we get there.'

She glanced at him, questioning her trust. 'It's a long shot.'

'It's all we have left. And a long shot came in once before, remember?'

'Okay. You're the boss.' She released the handbrake and accelerated off into the traffic.

She handled the little sports car with the skill of a racing driver. Weaving round container trucks, shaving red lights and making illegal use of bus lanes, they were soon out in open country. There, she treated the narrow roads as if they were the circuit at Brands Hatch, skidding to a halt outside the Portakabin in less than a quarter of an hour.

They rushed into the cabin and Naomi looked at Raven expectantly. 'Well, master? What now?'

To give himself time to think, he pointed at the tin of biscuits on top of the filing cabinet. 'A couple of chocolate digestives. And a cup of tea to wash 'em down.'

She made no effort to hide her disappointment. 'They sell biscuits in town, you know. And cups of tea.' But she handed him the biscuit tin and lit the gas under the kettle.

Raven sat down at Bill's desk and opened the chart of the caves. 'The answer's here somewhere,' he muttered, half to himself. 'It's just got to be.' Grabbing a big felt marker pen, he began to draw the outline round the entire system.

Naomi moved to stand at his shoulder, watching him. 'Do you think you should?' she asked doubtfully. 'That's Bill's official chart.'

Raven grinned up at her. 'Leave off. I'm Arthur, ain't I? The Dragon King.'

By the time she'd made the tea, he had finished. She handed him a cup, and they stared down at the primitive dragon he had drawn, sipping the hot liquid and trying to solve the mystery of the mythical beast. Why should the cave system have been designed in the shape of a dragon? It was obvious that the place had been planned with great care, so maybe the answer to the riddle lay in the network's outline.

'There's me dragon, right?' said Raven. 'Now – he's got eleven caves inside him, with eleven different signs above the entrances.'

'But there's twelve signs of the Zodiac,' said Naomi thoughtfully, 'and the one that's missing is Sagittarius.'

'You told me that was my sign.'

'Yes.'

'So where's me cave? Why haven't I got a cave, eh?'

Naomi studied the chart in silence for a moment. 'Sagittarius is a fire sign. The parent fire sign.'

'Fire…' Raven felt something stir in his mind like a sleeping giant. 'The Prof said Arthur was the Dragon King. And dragons breathe fire…'

'Go on,' said Naomi, saucer-eyed.

'And me symbol's the thing carved on the rock up there? Half horse, half man? What's it called?'

'A centaur.'

'Right. That's what we have to look for, then. Me dear old centaur…'

He moved the felt tip of the pen carefully round the dragon, searching for a shape within a shape.

'Centre,' said Naomi suddenly.

'I just said that.'

'No. Hang on a minute...' She grabbed the pen from him and drew the outline of the central core of rock through which Bill and his men had been tunnelling. 'See?'

Raven frowned at the plan. Why hadn't he seen it before? The central area was centaur-shaped, a man's body on a horse's legs.

Naomi rested her hand lightly on his shoulder. 'Suppose that rock-core turned out to be hollow?'

'The twelfth cave?'

'Which completes the Zodiac.'

Raven felt the giant-thought stir again. 'Entered through the dragon's mouth.'

Naomi leaned forward and stared intently at the chart. 'Yes!' she said excitedly, 'Yes, yes, yes, yes, yes, yes, yes. Nodes.'

'Yes, yes, yes, yes, yes, yes, no?'

'Nodes.' She pointed to the compass in the bottom left-hand corner. 'The degrees on the ecliptic where the moon moves from south to north latitude, or vice versa. In astrology, the South Node is called the Dragon's Tail, and the North Node the Dragon's Head... And here they are, see? South Node – North Node. In exactly the right positions. I told you – it's all in the stars.'

Raven stood up and peered at the Ordnance Survey map on the wall. 'So we go in here, right? Through Dragon's Teeth Ghyll...'

They stood facing each other, full of fearful wonder. What would they find behind the Dragon's Teeth? There was no time to summon help, which was probably how it was meant to be. Both of them knew instinctively that they would have to enter the beast's heart alone and unprotected. It was their destiny. As the Professor had said, what will come will come.

Chapter Twelve

AFTER THE TESTIMONY OF THE three Government experts, the Minister called a ten-minute recess. Castle and the Editor were standing outside the Council Chamber, sipping coffee from paper cups purchased from the refreshment trolley.

'Don't like the look of the old man,' said the Editor.

'Neither do I,' said Castle. 'He seems so – fragile. I doubt if he can stand up to a prolonged cross-examination.'

'Well, he's going to have to. Those boys from Whitehall sounded pretty convincing, and if our chief witness cracks, we'll have had it.'

The Minister approached, accompanied by Sir Lewis. 'I trust, Castle, that my colleagues' speeches will be fully reported in your programme?'

Castle gave him a sweet smile. 'Never trust anyone in television, Minister. Surely you've learned that by now?'

'If you don't give us coverage, you'll be making a fool of

yourself.'

'Why?'

'Because our side of the argument will appear in all the nationals. And your viewers are going to want to know why you alone ignored it.'

He turned and glided off into the Council Chamber with Sir Lewis in his wake.

The Editor crumpled his cup and threw it into a waste-paper basket. 'He's right, Clive.'

'I know.'

They wandered back to their seats in a pall of gloom. The Minister banged his gavel and called the meeting back to order. 'And now the case for the prosecution,' he said condescendingly, as if he were humouring a child. 'Professor Young?'

Mrs Young wheeled the old man forward, and two attendants lifted the chair onto the platform. Castle and the Editor gazed up at him in dismay: in the last few days he seemed to have shrunk in stature, and he suddenly looked like a wizened invalid, unable to cope with a world he no longer understood.

When he spoke, his voice was so weak it was barely audible. 'I am not qualified,' he began, 'to refute Sir Lewis's estimate of the project's safety precautions. That task I leave to my experts, who will tell you that, no matter how plausible the Government case might sound, it can never be a hundred per cent watertight. And if there is the slightest chance, however small, of some of the plutonium waste escaping by accident or theft, then the consequences for mankind would be so disastrous that the chance is not worth taking. The potential horror would outweigh all the benefits…'

He stopped and clutched his chest, his face contorted with pain. Castle and the Editor glanced at each other anxiously, but the spasm seemed to pass and the Professor continued as if nothing had happened.

'However, I am more concerned with the choice of this particular site. The protection of an ancient cave system that has not yet given up its secrets, whose ultimate mystery is still unsolved…'

He stopped and stared silently out of the window, his mind elsewhere. Castle shook his head dejectedly. 'He's not up to it,' he whispered to the Editor. 'Sir Lewis'll make mincemeat of him.'

The Editor glanced round at Raven and Naomi, and reacted with surprise when he saw that their seats were empty. 'Where are the kids?' he asked.

Castle shrugged. 'Probably swimming away from the sinking ship.'

'Then we've lost,' said the Editor. 'The boy's our last hope.'

*

The last hope was at that moment striding through wild, barren countryside, his eyes glued to the survey map. Naomi had to run to keep up with him, but she didn't complain: wherever he led, she was content to follow.

Suddenly, Raven came to an abrupt halt. They had reached the bottom of a hill about a mile away from the site, and the way ahead was blocked by a thick tangle of brambles and thorn-bushes.

He pocketed the map, took off his jacket and, holding it

in front of him as a shield, advanced slowly into the prickly undergrowth. The branches parted in front of him, clearing a path up the hillside.

They had climbed only a few yards when Raven stopped again. Facing them was a narrow cave-mouth, previously hidden by the foliage, with a steep incline leading downwards into darkness.

He turned. 'Give us the lamp.' Wordlessly, she handed him the lamp she had brought from the Portakabin, and followed him through the slit into the rock.

Raven held up the lamp and peered down the shaft into the impenetrable shadows below. 'Goes on forever,' he said grimly.

'Put the light out,' she told him.

'What?'

'Turn it off.' He switched off the lamp. 'Now – close your eyes and count to ten. One – two – three – four – five – six – seven – eight – nine – ten. All right, open!'

Raven opened his eyes and blinked. At first, the darkness was total and all-enveloping. Then, gradually, a flickering light became visible at the bottom of the shaft. 'Look,' he croaked hoarsely.

'It's fire,' she whispered, awed by the accuracy of their prediction.

'Yeah. The heart of the dragon . . .'

He took her hand and led her down the incline, carefully feeling ahead with his feet to make sure he didn't stumble over the small boulders that littered their path. The shaft grew steeper, but the light grew brighter, making it easier to see the obstacles in their way.

At the point where the incline became almost perpendicular, they came up against a rockface with a low archway at its base, etched in fire. The arch was blocked by a huge boulder, and the firelight came from a source beyond that flickered through the semi-circular crack around it, illuminating the primitive carving on its surface. It was a centaur.

'Can you shift it?' asked Naomi, sitting down to stop herself falling forward.

Raven pressed his back to the wall and shoved at the boulder with his feet. It rocked slightly. He tried again. This time the boulder moved appreciably before rolling back into place.

He was just about to try a third time, when his mind was suddenly filled with the sound of bells; a strange, unearthly music, infinitely beautiful, infinitely sad, that seemed to come from far away on the other side of the universe.

He paused for a moment, head on one side, listening. Naomi regarded him anxiously.

'What's the matter?'

'Dunno. Something's – going wrong.'

'What do you mean?'

He put his hands over his ears, but it made no difference. The sound increased in volume, its mysterious harmonies conjuring up shapeless phantoms in his memory. Then the phantoms dissolved, to be replaced by the image of the Professor resting his hand on the head of the stuffed merlin. The old man was smiling at him, and as the image receded, raised his arm in a gesture of farewell...

'It's the Prof,' said Raven suddenly. 'Something's happening to the Prof...'

*

The Professor sat slumped in his chair, wracked with pain. He had just managed to get through his evidence, but now he was at the end of his resources. Sir Lewis had re-entered the lists, and he was too old and tired to oppose him any longer.

'Let me see if I've got this right, Professor,' Sir Lewis was saying, his dry, sardonic voice cutting through the air like a knife. 'Your objection to the use of the cave system as a dumping ground is that it has not yet given up its secrets – whatever those might be – and that its ultimate mystery is still unsolved?'

'That's right.'

'Have you nothing more tangible to offer?'

'Tangible? How can there be anything tangible about… about the past?' He gasped and clutched his chest in agony.

Sir Lewis, head buried in a transcript of the Professor's speech, was too intent on driving home his point to notice his predicament. 'So you can't explain more fully why you think the cave system should be preserved?'

The Professor moaned softly and fell sideways in his chair. Mrs Young jumped to her feet in alarm and rushed onto the platform. But she was too late. Before she could reach her husband, he collapsed forward onto the floor.

The other officials ran to his aid, clustering round him like black crows. A ripple of sympathetic concern ran through the audience, and the Minister banged his gavel for silence.

'Please remain in your seats, ladies and gentlemen,' he called. 'I'm sure it's nothing serious. Probably just lack of air. Why don't we open a few more windows?'

The attendants did as he suggested, allowing a cool

breeze to blow through the Chamber. Castle and the Editor exchanged worried looks with Bill Telford and the vicar, sitting a few rows in front of them. All four rose and walked up onto the platform.

Two of the officials were trying to lift the Professor back into his chair, and Mrs Young was pleading with them to stop. 'No!' she was saying. 'Leave him where he is. He mustn't be moved till a doctor has examined him.'

'I'm a doctor.' One of the Professor's experts shouldered his way through the crowd. 'Stand back, please.'

He knelt down to examine the old man, while the vicar helped Mrs Young to a chair.

Bill, Castle and the Editor huddled in a little group at the corner of the platform. Stone joined them, looking lost and bewildered. 'That looked serious. How bad is it?'

'Dunno yet,' said Bill.

'What are we going to do if he has to go to hospital?'

'It's not up to us. It's up to the Minister.'

'That's right. It's my decision.' They turned as the Minister strolled up to them. He looked completely unconcerned, as if he thought the Professor's collapse was a put-up job. 'I hope you're capable of continuing without your leader?'

Castle looked at him with distaste. 'You mean you're not prepared to postpone this Appeal?'

''Fraid not. I'm a very busy man, you know. So are Sir Lewis and his colleagues. It might be months before we're all free again.'

'We're talking about centuries,' said Bill. 'And yet you can't even wait a few months?'

'We've waited long enough. We have to reach a

decision, so we know where we are. It's unfortunate about the Professor's illness or whatever it is, but time and tide wait for no man – not even him.'

Stone moved to stand in front of the Minister, eyes blazing. 'If you reach a decision without giving the Professor a chance to finish his evidence, you'll antagonise even more people than you have already.'

'The evidence he gave today was nothing new,' said the Minister. 'And if I may say so without offence, he was being remarkably unimpressive.'

'The man's obviously ill,' said Castle. 'Surely even you can see that?'

The Minister gave him a knowing smile. 'Is he?'

'What's that supposed to mean?'

'Just that his collapse came at a very convenient time.'

The men stared at him with loathing. The doctor stood up, looking grave, and walked slowly over to them.

'Well?' asked the Minister impatiently. 'What's the matter with him?'

'He's had a massive heart attack,' said the doctor quietly. 'I'm afraid he's dead.'

*

The distant bells died away into silence and the Professor's image faded into Naomi's face, lit by dancing fire.

'What was it you felt?' she asked anxiously. 'Some sort of premonition?'

Raven shook his head, puzzled and disturbed. 'Dunno.'

'You should always act on premonitions. I had one, remember – before the rockfall. We ought to go back.'

'No!' He was surprised by the authority in his voice.

'We've got a job to do. The best way we can help the Prof is by finishing it.'

'All right.' She indicated the boulder. 'Have another try.'

Raven sandwiched himself between the rock and the wall again and pushed.

'It's going!' said Naomi excitedly.

He rocked the boulder more and more violently, until it rolled away from its base and crashed down the shaft in a shower of rubble and dust. They peered through the gap in the rockface, and saw that the shaft led down into a small, irregular cave with a thick central column from floor to roof. The flickering light came from an opening near the top of the column, casting eery shadows onto the surrounding walls.

'This is it!' whispered Naomi in awed wonder. 'The twelfth cave!'

They slid down the shaft onto the floor of the cave and stared up at the rock-column in the centre. Carved into it, just below the opening, was the Pluto symbol.

'Gimme a leg up,' said Raven.

She made a cradle of her hands and he stepped into it, launching himself upwards. Grasping the bottom rim of the opening, he hauled himself slowly and painfully onto the ledge.

'Be careful,' Naomi called.

Raven stared through the opening and gasped with amazement. Inside the column was a tiny, circular area – a cave within a cave – filled with exquisitely jewelled stalagmites and stalactites, glittering and flashing like pointed stars. In the centre of the floor was the source of the flickering light – a great swordblade of burning gas.

Hypnotised by the flame, he struggled through the tiny aperture, and swung himself down to the ground. The gem-studded rock twinkled all around him, but he took no notice. Like a priest officiating at a religious ceremony, he advanced on the fiery sword, bent down and cupped it in his hands. Deprived of its flame, the gas hissed malevolently, beginning to fill the cave with poisoned air…

Outside the rock-column, Naomi waited, tense and frightened. From somewhere deep inside the cave system came the ancient sounds that had so disturbed Raven before – the stamping of horses' hooves, the jingling of a harness, ghostly laughter. Then, as the sounds died away, a more ominous noise – the hiss of escaping gas.

She called anxiously. 'Raven? Are you all right?'

He appeared at the aperture above her, gasping and spluttering, cupping a brilliant white light in his hands. He threw it down into the cave below, illuminating the cave in a brief, blinding flash – then collapsed onto the ledge, all his strength gone.

'Bring them to me,' he croaked hoarsely.

She stared up at him, transfixed with horror. 'Wait. Can't I…?'

'No. Get help. I need them here.'

She turned and scrambled back up the shaft on her hands and knees, sobbing with anxiety and frustration. She ran out of Dragon's Teeth Ghyll and stumbled down the hillside towards the construction site. Brambles clawed at her jeans, scratching her legs, but she hardly felt them.

By the time she reached the Portakabin, she was sick with exhaustion. Her hands were trembling so much that she tore the pages of the directory, and she had to dial three times before she got the correct number…

*

The Minister had just announced that the Hearing was adjourned. The public was filing out of the Council Chamber, appalled at the news of the Professor's death, and the witnesses on both sides stood about in disconsolate little groups, waiting for someone to tell them what to do.

A uniformed attendant walked up to Bill. 'Mr Telford? There's a call for you.'

Bill followed him out to the phone, and returned a moment later looking pale.

'It was Naomi,' he said to Castle and the others. 'Raven's trapped in the caves. She sounded a bit hysterical, but she mentioned something about gas.'

'Gas?' The Minister had overheard, and moved to join the group. 'There's no gas down there.'

'She's a responsible girl, Minister,' said the Editor. 'She wouldn't sound the alarm for no reason.'

'I'll fetch the rescue team,' said the vicar.

'Right.' Bill turned to the others. 'The rest of you with me.'

They hurried out of the room.

'Hang on,' called the Minister, 'I'm coming too.'

*

Naomi was waiting outside the Portakabin as the small fleet of cars screamed to a halt at the construction site.

'This way,' she said grimly, and started to lead the way across open moorland. The vicar and his men struggled after her, carrying their rescue equipment, and the camera crew, whom Castle had collected on his way out of the town hall, cursing under the weight of their heavy gear. The Minister brought up the rear, unloved and ignored, trying to look dignified while hurrying to keep up with the rest of the procession.

They reached Dragon's Teeth Ghyll and stumbled down the shaft into the cave. Raven was lying sprawled across the ledge at the top of the central column, half in and half out of the opening.

The vicar turned to his men. 'Get that scaling ladder up. He'll need the oxygen mask.'

Quickly and efficiently, they hauled the ladder into position. The Minister, seeing that Max's camera was already turning, grabbed the oxygen mask from the vicar and started to climb up to the unconscious Raven.

'Damn,' said Castle. 'Trust him to get into the act.'

The Minister lifted Raven's head and clamped the mask over his face. Raven stirred, brushed the mask away and stared at the Minister as if he were some terrible nightmare.

'Yeah,' he said. 'It's you I want.'

The Minister blinked at the Pluto-shaped mark on Raven's forehead and tried to clamp the mask back over his face. 'Don't worry, my boy,' he said for the benefit of the camera, 'I'll save you.'

'No you won't, mate. I'll save you.' Raven grabbed the Minister by the lapels and pulled his head into the gas-filled inner cave.

The Minister cried out in sudden panic. 'Raven! What are you doing?'

He twisted his head away to try and escape the gas, but Raven held on inexorably and he felt himself slipping into unconsciousness. A strange series of images burst into his mind – Raven as a young king stretching out his thumb towards his forehead in a slow-motion, ritual gesture… an astrological symbol burning through his brain like a brand… and a huge atomic explosion that mushroomed inside his head, a terrifying glimpse of a future holocaust. It was to be a vision he would remember for the rest of his life.

*

'I still don't understand how Raven did it,' Stone was saying. 'When the Minister reached ground level, he was a changed man.'

'Something to do with the gas?' suggested Bill.

'Maybe.'

'Well, ours not to reason why. Let's just be grateful it's the end of the project.'

They were down in the caves – Bill, Stone, Castle, the Editor, the vicar and the five experts – celebrating their victory with champagne. There would be no nuclear reprocessing plant – the Minister had made the announcement at the top of the lift shaft – and the ancient site could rest in peace.

In another part of the complex, Naomi was searching for Raven. He had come down with them, but had disappeared soon after the party began. She was worried: he had hardly spoken all day, and now it seemed as if he were avoiding her.

To say goodbye to him would not be easy. She was aware of the pain in his heart, but she hoped there was no bitterness. When she'd told Clive that she wanted to be alone with him for a moment, he had immediately understood: he, too, had once been sixteen.

She found him in the Libran cave, standing quite still. There was a slight smile on his face, as if he were listening to some faraway music. The smile faded as he saw her, and the dark eyes that watched her walk up to him were expressionless.

'I have to go, Raven,' she said quietly. 'You know that, don't you? It's what I've always wanted to do…'

She paused, waiting for him to say something, but he remained staring at her, silent and motionless. She realised with a start that she had become a little afraid of him. The boy had become a man of unmistakeable authority and power.

'I knew it the moment I saw him,' she went on awkwardly. 'Please try to understand. You and me – it was never on, love… it would never have worked.'

The smile returned, tender and sad. They looked at each other for a long moment, dry-eyed.

'Anyway, I'm going. Spreading my wings. Wish me luck?'

He shut his eyes, unable to look at her any more. She touched his pale, finely chiselled face, turned and walked away. If ever they met again, it would be as strangers.

Epilogue

RAVEN SAT ON THE HILL above the little churchyard, watching the Professor's funeral. The black figures below were clustered round the graveside like a colony of beetles. Soon they, too, would die and return to Mother Earth. Ashes to ashes, dust to dust…

The vicar had tried to persuade him to attend the ceremony. 'For Mrs Young's sake,' he had said. 'I'm sure she'd want you to be there.' But the old man had meant too much to him. He wanted to be alone – to say farewell in his own way.

The coffin was lowered, and the mourners scattered earth onto the lid. The air was calm and still, with a touch of autumn in it, and the vicar's resonant voice drifted lazily up the hillside. 'He was a great man. Guide, philosopher and friend. Respected by all, but known only to a few…'

He took Mrs Young's arm and led her down the path to a waiting car. Her face was covered with a veil, but from the way her shoulders heaved Raven knew she was crying. He felt like crying himself, but the tears refused to come.

One by one, the mourners climbed into their cars and drove away. When the last of them had gone, the vicar signalled to the gravediggers standing unobtrusively by the side of the church. The men walked up to the grave and began to shovel earth into it.

The vicar walked back up the path – stopped, glanced up at Raven and raised his hand in a silent salute – then disappeared into the church. Raven waited, his hair ruffled by the breeze, knowing that though the formalities had been completed, the ceremony was not yet over…

*

As soon as she got back to the house, Mrs Young went straight into the study and lit a fire. When it had burnt up into a crackling blaze, she took the case off the stuffed merlin, carried the bird over to the fireplace and threw it on the flames. She watched without emotion as feathers, beak and talons were charred into ashes…

*

All through the afternoon, Raven maintained his lonely vigil. Just before sunset, the vicar left the church and drove away. The gravediggers had long since finished their work, leaving behind a neat rectangle of newly dug earth.

Suddenly, as the sun disappeared behind the trees and the shadows lengthened across the graveyard, the earth began to tremble and heave. Raven stood up expectantly.

A blue-and-yellow bird struggled out of the earth into the light. It shook its wings, then soared up into the sky.

Raven watched it circle once round the graveyard, then fly off towards the setting sun.

He stood motionless until the dark speck dipped over the horizon – a young king in the middle of an empty domain. Finally satisfied, he turned and strode away across his land.